Girl in the Tapestry

by Virginia Harris Hendricks

Heartwood Press ~ Austin, Texas

The publisher is:
  Heartwood Press
  3305 Stardust Drive
  Austin, Texas 78757
  HeartwoodP@aol.com

ISBN: 0-9661605-0-9
Library of Congress Catalog Card Number: 98-96134

Printed and bound in the U.S.A.

LOVINGLY DEDICATED TO:

MARGIE,
MARY,
SARAH

AND

JOANNA,
KATIE,
RUTH

My Sincere Thanks To:

Aubusson, its mayor, and its superintendent at the Tapestry Works at the time I visited, collecting information for this book.

To my friend and language tutor, Jacqueline (Jackie), who introduced me to Aubusson and to proper French.

To the many friends who have read my manuscript through the years and believed in it.

To my family who believe in *me*. Especially to Bill, my husband and true love, who put up with late nights and frayed nerves, who did the dishes and kept the fire burning, to make this happen.

To Jess and Doris Moody who have been on my side, regardless.

To my publisher and editors who brought my dream to reality.

Chapter I
Girl in the Tapestry

Julie swooped down the circular staircase in the castle tower as usual, her bright pink skirts billowing out behind her, her dark brown hair bouncing about her shoulders. As she reached the second floor, she remembered the serious nature of her mission and slowed her steps to a sedate pace, appropriate for a young gentlewoman of sixteen who had been formally summoned by her uncle the Count of Valjean.

The Chateau Valjean perched on a hill overlooking the Cher River, nineteen miles east of Orleans. When Julie arrived here with her mother five years ago, her uncle's imposing stone castle overwhelmed her. It stretched up into the sky, and its twin towers stood like tall sentinels facing the river.

When her mother died a few months after their arrival, her uncle moved Julie to the front third floor bedroom and sitting room apartment. From her windows, Julie could see over the treetops and river to the green countryside and dark forests beyond. One of the two tower stairways provided an almost private entrance to her apartments from the courtyard. Her aunt preferred that Julie use the great hall staircase, but Julie loved the little winding stairs that led from her sky-high rooms.

"Little did I know that I would be spending my sixteenth birthday in this place," mused Julie aloud as she swished slowly down the remaining steps. "I'm beginning to believe that Father will never bring me home to Aubusson, else he would've answered my letters or sent for me."

The thought returned to her that this summons could be an answer to her plea to visit her father. She skipped down the last few steps two at a time.

The tower ended with two exits: one going outdoors to the courtyard, the other into the big drawing room. As she paused at the outdoor exit, Julie saw her seventeen-year-old cousin, Albert, dismount from his dark gray mare in the October drizzle.

Francois, two years older than Albert, had already dismounted and came striding toward the door. He brushed Julie aside in his rush to get indoors.

"Give me time and I'll move," she protested.

Francois removed his hat and folded his cloak neatly over his arm. Barely looking at her, he muttered, "You're always in my way." He swaggered up the stairs.

Albert entered, discarding hat, rain cape, jacket, and boots at the doorway. He flung these garments toward the pegs in the wall, ignoring the wet wraps as they missed the pegs and slid to the floor.

"You should've gone with us, Julie," Albert exclaimed. "If we leave for Paris as planned, there are few days left for riding in Orleanaise."

"Riding wildly about the countryside is not an appropriate way for a young lady to celebrate her sixteenth birthday," Julie mimicked her aunt's precise voice. "Besides, I'm no longer allowed to wear breeches for riding. The sport isn't fun in these." Julie's skirts rustled softly as she pivoted around on her toes.

"And what are we doing to celebrate this ninth day of October, sixteen eighty-five?" Albert's hand on her arm guided Julie towards the drawing room door.

"First, 'we' are making a command appearance before the count," answered Julie.

"Not one of those!" Albert winced as he stepped aside for Julie to precede him into the large drawing room.

"Oh, that tapestry!" gasped Julie. "Where did it come from? Whose is it?"

"That? Papa admired it in Paris but couldn't get the owner to sell it. Then last night someone brought it to Papa as a gift."

"A gift? I think I know that tapestry." Julie couldn't take her eyes off of the woven wall hanging of glowing, rich colors that was as wide as the tremendous fireplace underneath it.

"You talk as if it's human," laughed Albert.

"Can that really be the tapestry in my memory? Surely, it's the same golden-haired damsel protecting the wounded fawn from that handsome bewildered hunter. And see? Here is the strange fish signature of the designer in the left corner."

"You know the designer? Papa's friend says it's a mystery." Albert looked at Julie with raised eyebrows.

"No, I've wondered about the designer like everyone else. I believe the Count of Aubusson knew. It hung in his chateau when I was small. I think it's the most magnificent tapestry in the world!" Julie's enthusiasm amused her cousin.

"Well, I see nothing remarkable about the tapestry, and I can't see why everyone else gets so excited over it," Albert said.

"It's the girl who's so remarkable, Albert." Julie insisted. "It's amazing that a fabric weaving can portray such an expressive face. Even you can see the setting must be a royal hunting forest. I can imagine two horses tethered on opposite sides, out of sight behind the trees, and..."

"Oh, no! Not another lecture on tapestries, please," Albert teased Julie about her obsession for tapestries.

"Stop it, cousin!" Julie laughed. "Can I help it if my father is one of the greatest tapestry artisans in France?"

"Better remember that your mother was a de Beaulac." Albert was no longer teasing.

"You don't understand how important this tapestry is to me. It hung in the home of my father's dearest friend in Aubusson, and my friend, too," Julie added, as she remembered her childhood idol, Philippe de Vauve.

Philippe was four years older than she. It was curious that he had tolerated the little girl who shadowed him in the village where they grew up together.

"Philippe and I used to make up stories about the picture. He loved to make me mad by saying that he was going to marry that girl when he grew up."

The beautiful girl in the tapestry seemed like an old friend, rediscovered, as Julie gazed up at her. It was strange that Albert, always interested in a pretty face, was so unimpressed.

The tapestry released memories that increased her homesickness for Aubusson. Memories surfaced of the carefree days spent playing and studying with Philippe, of the hum and clack of the shuttles as her father and his weavers worked busily at the looms. She especially remembered the face of the great, loving man of her childhood, her father.

"The count allowed me to study under Philippe's tutor. He declared that even though I was a girl, I deserved a chance to learn from books." Julie turned to face Albert. "So that's why I'm such a 'bookworm' and 'school girl', two names you love to call me."

Julie then noticed that Albert was paying little attention to her or the tapestry. She wished that something more substantial than good times and pocket money interested Albert or Francois. She knew they both resented her wider knowledge. It wasn't fashionable for aristocratic young ladies to be intelligent, especially not more intelligent than the men they were supposed to pursue.

Albert had heard more than Julie thought. He turned from the window and shook his finger mockingly at her. "Let me give you a bit of advice, dear cousin. Don't let on that this tapestry means anything to you. In particular, don't say it was ever in Aubusson. Papa saw it in the Paris house of the older de Vauve son, now Count of Aubusson." Albert shrugged his shoulders and turned away. "Remember, it's your birthday, and if you play it smart, the tapestry might become yours."

Julie grabbed his arm. "Albert, do you think that's possible?"

"Not unless you watch your tongue. And, by all means, agree with the old man when he talks to you. Be a nice, obedient girl, and there is no telling what the future will bring." Albert's cupped Julie's chin in his hand, his face too near her own. His eyes were cold and calculating. Julie shivered. Albert was changing from the fun-loving boy who had been her playmate.

Julie withdrew hastily. She started toward her uncle's library, which was next to the drawing room. "I'd give almost anything to own that tapestry," she said.

"Wait!" he stopped her. "I didn't say that you were getting the tapestry. I was just saying you might get it by being agreeable. Actually, the tapestry is a symbol of an alliance between Papa and a rather important person from Paris."

Julie's ambitious uncle was always working on some scheme to improve his social or financial standing. Her aunt prodded him on. Of course, this was necessary for survival in the society in which they liked to move. Either you had connections with King Louis the Fourteenth's court, or you were nobody.

Before Julie reached the library door, her aunt unexpectedly came through it. Julie thought she glimpsed a visitor in the room before her aunt closed the door.

"Wait a moment, dear. The count isn't quite ready for you," the countess said. Her dainty manner always made Julie feel less than feminine.

"Now that Julie is sixteen, we must all realize that we have a grown young lady in our family and behave accordingly." The countess declared, addressing Albert.

"I don't think Julie wants to be grown-up and proper. She withers every young swain who tries to make an impression," Albert said.

"When we go to Paris again, we will arrange for Julie to appear at King Louis' court, and she will dazzle and be dazzled." Her aunt seemed sure of herself.

"I was hoping I would be allowed to visit Aubusson before I go to Paris," Julie said.

"I have carefully trained you for the life you will lead now." The countess ignored the reference to Aubusson, but her voice was harder. "We shall be very proud of you, won't we? You will be the loveliest, most sought after court lady of them all."

"Aunt Isabelle, I don't think I'm suited for court life. You know how unimpressed I was with those two absurd young ladies you invited here last summer. If they represent court society, I shall be bored and disgusted with Paris."

"Julie! I forbid you to insult my friend's daughters. You're so foolish. I had hoped you would learn gracious living from them. I have given you a mother's love and the most careful training since your own poor mother died. After seeing the life she was forced to lead with that ignorant man she married, how can you refuse the life that she missed?"

"Ignorant! My father is not ignorant! He is educated and nobly born, too, remember, and followed an artist's life by choice." Julie surprised even herself by this unusual defense of a parent whom she hadn't seen or heard from for nearly five years. The tapestry had bewitched her.

The countess blinked back angry tears from her pale eyes, then turned sharply on her high heels and strutted from the room.

Albert frowned. "You don't believe in following advice, do you? Watch it, Julie!" He entered the tower, and Julie heard him stomping up the stairs to his room, directly above.

Left standing in the middle of the room, Julie pressed a clenched fist to her lips. Was she really ungrateful to her aunt and uncle? True, they had bought her elegant clothes and provided excellent teachers of social behavior. She knew it must have been trying for her fragile aunt to tame a wild, young outdoors girl who had not particularly wanted to become a fine lady. Why should she feel so rebellious, and why could she no longer hide her rebellion?

Julie faced the tapestry again. The sight of the golden girl in the weaving compelled her to cry out, "Am I an ungrateful niece?" In a whisper, she added, "or an unfaithful daughter?"

Julie had at last voiced the question that tormented her. She knew that life in Aubusson would be different for a grown young lady than for a spirited child. Perhaps she could never adjust to such a life again. But Julie felt that in Aubusson she had possessed a genuine happiness that had escaped her since she and her mother fled.

Julie usually slammed a door in her mind when memories of that flight returned to haunt her. The tapestry had strongly affected her, however, and she could no longer shut away the vivid memory of a dark, frantic child and her beautiful, pleading mother.

Her father had been summoned to a tapestry fair at Lyons to represent his village. Before he left, he took his daughter aside. Julie remembered his words clearly, for they were his last to her.

"Julie, ma cherie. I must leave for a few days, and I'm worried. Your mother is worse. Will you take good care of her, Julie? Be gentle and loving, and please her while I'm gone. One day she will be the happy, beautiful lady whom I brought to Aubusson long ago. Her sickness will go away. It must!" Julie could still see his deep-set, compassionate dark eyes.

Girl in the Tapestry

All her life Julie had felt protective toward her fragile, child-like mother. Taking her cue from her father, she had shielded and spoiled the woman who clung to her unhappiness as though it were a precious garment. When they were alone, her mother talked incessantly of the carefree life at Valjean, of the parties she had attended in Paris, and of the time the Sun King, Louis himself, had spoken to her.

When the strange carriage decorated with the Valjean crest appeared, Julie's mother pleaded and cried and even threatened to leave Aubusson without her. Julie decided that her duty demanded she care for her mother as her father had charged her, even if it tore her away from her cottage home. Her child's heart ached with fear and uncertainty as the fine horses pulled them away. Her reverie ended with the usual bitter realization that her father had never forgiven her: he had never sent to bring her home.

A noise from the next room reminded Julie of her summons. She now faced it with dread, for she no longer hoped for good news about Aubusson. What had Albert been hinting? And why had her aunt been so upset with her?

Chapter II
Plot Against Julie

The library door opened, and the count stood framed in the doorway. Julie thought him especially handsome in his bright blue waistcoat with white ruffles at the wrists. She was painfully aware of her own undisciplined tresses as she noted that her uncle was wearing his best black wig. What occasion called for such elegance? Certainly not a niece's birthday.

She glided across the room and stopped in front of him. Sorry now for the outburst that distressed her aunt, Julie said, "Uncle Claude, you and Aunt Isabelle have been wonderful to me. I suppose a birthday is as good a time as any to tell you so, and to say that I'm grateful."

At her words, his eyes sparkled, and Julie wished that she had expressed her appreciation more often. His next words rekindled her apprehension.

"Julie, my dear, how seriously you talk. Why, you're a daughter to us, and I always have your best welfare in mind." His eyes twinkled as if hiding some delightful surprise, but when they met Julie's eyes, he nervously looked away. He continued, "I know you realize that since you are now sixteen, it's time to discuss your future."

He led her into the library. First he glanced sideways at her, then away. He stuck his hands into his waistcoat pockets and pretended interest in something outside the open garden door. From this door trickled the only light which penetrated the dark, musty room. Julie wondered why the window curtains were still closed.

The count suddenly spun around and extended his arms in a dramatic gesture. "In short, my dear Julie, it's time we announced your marriage engagement."

"But I'm not ready to be married!" she exploded.

"Keep your voice down, Julie, and don't act so surprised." "Why did her uncle seem so nervous?" Julie wondered. "You're teasing me, Uncle Claude," she said, hoping this was true.

"I've never been more serious in my life. At sixteen, desirable young ladies are usually publicly engaged, and you know it. We've avoided a confrontation with you, but you've been unofficially engaged for several months. One of the most successful, eligible men in France asked for your betrothal three years ago. He was accepted, of course."

"Accepted by whom?" demanded Julie.

"By myself!" The count's impatience intensified. He towered over his rather tall niece. "Let me remind you of a few facts, young lady. In the first place, we've given you a home and training to prepare you for this very day. It has always been our intention to marry you into an eminent family, to a man who can support you lavishly. Since my agreement with your intended, he and I have both made commitments. Some of the advantages I have already received, including my new position at the king's court. There is no point in acting stubborn with me, for everything is arranged, and you are going through with it!"

"It cannot be!" Julie protested.

"Why, you haven't even asked me the name of your suitor," exclaimed the count.

"I have no suitor!" Julie's temper flared against her uncle. Usually he enjoyed their arguments, but this was, no doubt, the most serious alliance he had ever made. Julie could see he was determined that nothing would spoil it.

"Will you let me tell you his name? Then we will see how much you object. Every girl in France would envy a marriage to the Marquis Louis de Feuillarde!" Her uncle sounded triumphant, sure these magic words would melt her resistance.

Julie stared in disbelief; she couldn't speak for shock. The marquis was the most conceited man she knew and old enough to be her father. True, the Marquis had been exceptionally kind to her, but she had always resented his attentions. Now she understood why. He had acted as though he had claim on her all these months, and she could see why his attitude had repelled her.

"I will enter into no marriage betrothal without my father's permission." Julie was grasping at straws.

"I am your legal father," her uncle reminded her.

"You are not! My father, my only father, is in Aubusson."

"I am your legal guardian. Your father is a Protestant heretic. Therefore the government recognizes me as your lawful guardian."

Julie knew that the laws punished those who dared to defy the state church. She knew that the state could seize the children of Protestants.

"Then I declare myself a Protestant, and it's illegal for a Protestant to marry a Catholic!"

Julie's uncle had always shown affection toward her, and the hateful gleam in his narrowed eyes alarmed her.

"You are never to speak those words again! You are Catholic. Your mother secretly took you to the monastery chapel in Aubusson for baptism when you were only a few days old. Your mother risked her life by leaving her bed to take you there."

Julie opened her mouth to speak, but her uncle motioned her into silence. "Your father came to this chateau twenty-five years ago. Under my very nose, he made my young sister fall in love with him. In spite of all I did, she went away with this man, who is not only beneath her in family rank but an enemy of our church and king. Any man who leaves his title of nobility to become an artisan and who persists in supporting heretical teachings is no better than a dog! If it weren't for his exceptional skill in his field, he would have been destroyed long ago. In fact, his fate will ... " He stopped, then continued. " I forbid you to utter his name, ever again, or to admit any relation to him for your own safety!"

"But Jacques de Mirovar *is* my father!" Julie sobbed.

"Let me jar you out of this nonsense, young lady!" The count leaned one arm upon a heavily carved bookcase. He adjusted his wig slightly with his other hand. "To profess the Huguenot faith means death, or worse. You were never told that your father's parents were executed and his brother sent to sea as a galley slave after Flanders came under the French crown, all because the de Mirovars refused to renounce the Huguenots. The only thing that spared Jacques was the king's desire to bring expert Flemish tapissiers to develop the French industry. You're very fortunate that your mother was a de Beaulac."

Julie shook her head slightly to clear her dazed mind. Then she drew herself up stiffly before her uncle. Her tall, agile frame, the product of natural grace and a lifetime of horseback riding, couldn't begin to convey her outrage.

"You will see the marquis today. You will submit to our plans and behave like a nobly born gentlewoman," he declared.

"But I despise the Marquis de Feuillarde!" Her uncle's sudden agitation encouraged her. "I'd rather marry that, that ... couch over there!" Julie waved her arm toward the love seat in the window alcove. Her arm froze in midair. Beneath the portable Chinese screen that now hid the love seat, she spied a pair of shiny black boots.

"Who's there?" she asked. Someone chuckled behind the screen, and a short, impeccably dressed man strutted forth. He wore an elaborate red wig, long curls cascading over his shoulders. His black mustache was carefully trimmed and waxed. His thin mouth smiled, but his black eyes didn't.

"The more I see and, ahem, hear you, my dear Lady Juliet, the more I congratulate myself on my farsightedness in choosing you for my own. Not every man would have seen in a mere child the young woman-to-be. I must say, it was rather wise of me to choose you so young, for even though your education for court life has been the best we can offer, I can see there are certain manners that need more attention."

Julie looked about for her uncle. She was dismayed to see that he had disappeared. The marquis walked around her, looking her over with approval stamped on his face.

"Hmmm, can't say your natural gifts need any improvement, other than the most fashionable clothes money can buy and some tasteful hair arranging. Ah, Julie, what a pair we shall make!"

"You act as though you were choosing a horse rather than a wife, Monsieur!" she retorted, haughtily.

"And what is wrong with that, if the filly is spirited, beautiful, and worthy of my ownership? I've mastered and trained some of the most handsome horses in France."

"You eavesdropped on my conversation with my uncle." Julie glared at the marquis. "Don't you realize that I have no intention of marrying you?"

"You've been reading too many romantic tales, my lovely. It's bad for a woman to read so much. Real love is quite different from love as described in novels. You will learn to adore me, I assure you. You will grace my household as my beautiful, desirable wife. Right now, you're acting like a spoiled child. You don't realize all that I'm offering you. If you did, you would be throwing yourself into my arms and ... Ah, but then you wouldn't be Julie."

Julie was furious. Everyone was convinced that she already belonged to this despicable man.

"I'm quite mature enough to know that marriage with you would be a wretched life!" she hissed.

"You are a hot little rebel." the marquis exclaimed. He no longer smiled. "It's that Huguenot blood that courses in your veins. I shall destroy that rebellion in you, even as I have destroyed hordes of those heretics. I shall remake you, Julie, so help me!"

Julie ducked nimbly away as the marquis snatched at her, his eyes gleaming maliciously, his mouth twisted. The marquis pursued her as she dashed into the drawing room on her way to the tower. Once in the tower, she scanned frantically for a weapon. There was nothing in sight except Albert's riding garments. Desperately, she grabbed these from the floor. She fled up the stairway, the marquis in close pursuit. Without even pausing, she tossed the balled up clothing expertly at the marquis' boots. He tripped and sprawled down several steps, yelping with anger and surprise.

"Come back here, you little vixen!" he shouted as he scrambled to his feet to continue his pursuit. Julie now had a good lead. She raced into her room at the top of the stairs and bolted the door behind her.

"Open that door this instant!" screamed the enraged marquis. "How dare you resist me?"

She backed against the opposite wall, her frightened eyes on the shaking door, her heart pounding. The man was a maniac. And her uncle, who she had thought loved her, had promised her, no, sold her, to such a person.

She heard voices outside. Her uncle tried to soothe the angry aristocrat. "I know, I know," he said. "You are indeed the man who can subdue my niece, but please, dear friend, compose yourself. Have patience. We shall arrange the marriage date for whenever you say."

Julie couldn't catch the mumbled answer. Then her uncle spoke again. "She's just a young girl, overwhelmed by the attentions of such an important official. She will be very anxious to go through with the marriage. How can she help it?"

She could imagine how easily the conceited marquis would fall for that idea. But she would never, never marry him. Never!

As the footsteps of the two men died away, Julie buried her face in her arms. She couldn't understand how her family could force her into such a hateful alliance. Uncle Claude was more ambitious than she had realized. Of course, the expense of the estate here, as well as the town house in Paris, strained his purse, and he could pay for their upkeep only through the court appointment that the marquis must have arranged.

Perhaps her cousins would also profit from the proposed connection with the marquis' family. It was rumored that the marquis was more wealthy than the king himself. In fact, according to gossip around the Valjean dining table, this was the secret of his influence at court. Many stories also circulated about how he had accumulated this wealth, none of them complimentary to the marquis. Much of his fortune had come from an early marriage. When his rich wife died, from poison, some suspected, he never remarried.

"I must get out of this place. I've got to escape." she muttered to herself. "But there's no one to help, except maybe Albert."

Escape seemed impossible. Julie had never been allowed to go alone off the estate. She rode with her cousins, she shopped in Orleans and Paris with friends and her aunt, and, for some time, she had never been left alone in town. These restrictions, which had seemed like loving protection, now obviously had a more sinister purpose.

A rap at the door startled her. "Who is it?"

"Friend, not foe." came a familiar voice.

"Oh, Albert!" She threw open the bolt and pulled her cousin into her room. "I'm so glad you came to me. I feel like the whole world is against me."

Albert carried his riding clothes bundled under his arm. He tossed them on the bench under the window and teased, "Who's been scattering my clothes all over the stairs?"

"They saved me, Albert, from a mad animal." Julie said.

"I know, I heard all about it." His laugh sounded hollow.

"Oh, Albert, what am I going to do?" she wailed.

He slouched into a dainty chair and frowned. His blue eyes wouldn't meet hers. "I didn't know you had any choice, cousin."

Julie was stunned to think Albert was siding against her. He squirmed under her shocked gaze, then went on.

"Now, look. Let's be reasonable. You have your whole life ahead of you, and look what's being offered. Everything a woman could want. I wish somebody would give me a chance to marry such a fortune. In fact, Julie, there is a chance that I can win the marquis' niece after you two are married."

She looked intently at her cousin. "Do you know this niece?"

"Well, no. But it would be a great opportunity for me, if we can swing it."

"But I won't marry this beast!" She spit the last word out. "I would rather go back to Aubusson!"

Albert returned Julie's scrutiny. "You haven't got a chance. Papa ended all your connections with Aubusson years ago. Forget it."

She wanted to hear more about ended connections. "Maybe he thinks he has ended connections, but maybe I've fooled him." Julie watched him closely for his reaction. Albert bolted upright in the chair.

"Has your father gotten a letter through to you?"

"What makes you think we don't write regularly?" she asked, hiding her startled excitement.

"Aha! Not regularly, for Papa won't allow it. In fact, I think you're teasing. Papa's men watch every stranger passing through. Don't you realize that they would kidnap you if we didn't protect you so carefully?"

Julie desperately wanted more information from him. Though the news of her uncle's censorship made her shake with fury, she said nothing. Albert misinterpreted her silence and her shocked stare.

"I mean it. Right now, there is an officer from Aubusson at the inn, on convalescence he says, but he's watched for your sake."

"I don't know any soldiers from Aubusson," she said.

"Of course you don't. I'm just trying to show you how careful Papa is. If somebody is from that part of the country, he's kept away from Valjean."

"You mean the soldier tried to come here?"

Albert became alert. "I'm not even supposed to be talking about Aubusson. Just take my advice and forget about that place. From what I hear, your father is headed for trouble, and you would be, too, if you were with him!"

He rose and strode to the door leading into the big hall. His next words convinced her that he had been sent to change her attitude.

"Julie, you're very lucky. You could still be buried in a dull village someplace, but Papa rescued you from all that. You've been given the best education, for one purpose: to decorate the king's court and the house of the marquis as his wife. You can rise as high as you want to, with your beauty and personality. You're not from the same mold as the average court decoration. Take my advice and go along with the plans. Please."

Julie said nothing. Albert fidgeted a moment then turned and left her room, forgetting to take the clothes he had brought. She drew his cloak to her face, inhaling the fragrance of the outdoors, the smell of the horses.

"Oh, Albert! You, too, are one of them!" Julie hit the bundle of clothing with her fist. Then she rummaged into the folds and pulled out his hunting knife. She tossed it on the floor and continued to sob into the cloak, pounding it from time to time with both fists.

"'Education', they all say! My only 'education' in this place is how to preen like a court lady, how to flirt with conceited men like the marquis, how to talk and say nothing, and how to deceive my own family. My real education stopped when I left Aubusson!"

Chapter III
Stairway to Danger

Julie sat upright on the window bench, startled by a noise at the tower door. She realized that she hadn't bolted the lock after admitting Albert and sprang toward the slowly opening door. Before she could slam it shut, she saw the gray muslin skirt and soft brown slippers of Felicie, the servant girl who worked downstairs. She was balancing a pewter tray on her left hand. It held a spoon, a jug of steaming liquid, and a cloth-covered plate.

"Why didn't you knock?" demanded Julie.

Felicie glanced at the tear-stained face of the mistress, then walked to a teak wood table where she placed her load. Her speech carried the broad accent of the Orleannais.

"Mademoiselle, I'm not supposed to be here. But nobody sent you any lunch, and I thought you should have something."

This thoughtfulness surprised Julie, for she had very little to do with the downstairs maid. It was a wonder that she even recalled the girl's name.

"Where is Ularie?" Julie hadn't seen her own maid since early morning.

"She was told to take a few days off and was sent home." Felicie uncovered a small platter of stew and poured a cup of steaming chocolate.

"Ularie told me to see that you got something to eat," Felicie added, "because she didn't leave you by choice. It's plain the master wants you to be alone." Felicie looked fearfully toward the door.

"I'm not hungry. However, since you risked so much to come, I'll try to eat." Julie smiled as she took the spoon and tasted the spicy stew.

"Am I banished from all meals with the family?" Julie asked, her spoon in midair.

"Yes, Mademoiselle." She seemed afraid to say more.

"Felicie, please tell me what's going on downstairs. I feel so abandoned, so alone." Julie's eyes brimmed with tears, and these tears melted Felicie's caution. She decided to risk telling Julie all she knew.

"Well, now," Felicie fluttered around her, "Justine served the gentlemen at lunch. He says that the marquis is set upon an early wedding. He aims to announce the engagement as soon as he gets back to Paris. Your aunt wanted to get a grand trousseau and wedding clothes and all that, but the marquis says he will buy everything. He says there must be no putting off."

"Go on."

"The servants were all called together and we were told to keep you from leaving this chateau. Ularie was sent away because she refused to spy on you for the family." Felicie stopped.

"I wonder why I haven't been locked in?"

"The family hopes you will repent and rejoin them, after some time alone. There are guards below."

"Is that all you can tell me?" Julie asked gently.

Felicie shook her head. "The servants overheard a lot. They are worried about you. They ..."

Julie walked over and put her arm around Felicie's shoulders. "I don't know why you should risk so much for me, Felicie. You have no idea how much I appreciate what you've told me. But, please, if there is more I should know, don't keep it from me."

"They ... they talked about how they would make you go through with the wedding. And the marquis says he has got to have a big Paris wedding because he has all the court expecting it. But the family knows how stubborn you are." Felicie glanced anxiously at Julie, who nodded encouragement.

"If you refuse to cooperate with the wedding plans, the marquis said not to worry, he knows a good chemist, and he's sure that with certain drugs he can take away your 'fire and spirit' – that's what he said – during the ceremony. After that ..." Felicie looked fearfully at the mistress.

Julie returned to the chair beside the little table. She attacked her lunch with new determination. Felicie fidgeted, twisting her hands in her apron. Julie sensed Felicie's stare. She finished the stew and turned toward her.

"Felicie, do you know any Huguenots?"

Felicie snatched the empty platter, and it clattered noisily as she put it on the pewter tray. Her frightened eyes never strayed from the doorway as she frowned. "Why ever would you ask me a question like that? There are no Huguenots around here."

"Are you sure, Felicie? They are my only hope. I've heard of how they help fugitives escape."

"What makes you think they would help you? Their own kind, maybe ..."

"But, Felicie, I am a Huguenot!" Julie whispered fiercely.

Felicie stared in disbelief. "You couldn't be. This house ..." She said no more. Julie grabbed Felicie's dress as she abruptly started for the doorway, anxious to leave.

"Felicie, did you ever hear of the famous tapestry maker Jacques de Mirovar, who renounced his title and lost his lands and family because of his Huguenot faith?"

"What's that got to do with you?" Felicie wasn't committing herself to knowledge of Huguenots.

"He's my father!" announced Julie. "That is why I'm kept a

prisoner here, and why I cannot marry the marquis." She had no idea why she was telling Felicie so much. "Oh, Felicie, I want to go to my father in Aubusson. Is there no one who can help me?"

Felicie stood in the middle of the room, holding the tray. Julie could see that she was upset and undecided.

"If I did know any Huguenots and told you about them, do you know I'd be risking their lives?" she said.

"I'd lose my own life before I would betray them," Julie answered.

Felicie started to speak, then stopped. Finally, she said, "If you could get out of this chateau, which I doubt, I might tell you of a Huguenot house."

"Oh, Felicie! Felicie! I must get out of this place! I shall!" Disregarding the tray, Julie threw her arms around the girl. "Please, oh, please tell me. You're my only hope."

Felicie rescued the tumbling bowl before it reached the floor. She hesitated again, but Julie's pleas paid off.

"Listen carefully. Do you know the farm of Joel Vagran about two miles down the river road toward Orleans?"

Julie puckered her brow and rubbed the nape of her neck.

"With a good stone stable, thatched roof house, and the ruins of an old tower?" Felicie added.

"Yes, yes," Julie nodded eagerly. "I've ridden by there many times. They have a little boy named Henri who sometimes waters our horses for us, and I give him bonbons."

"If you stop there, they might tell you where to find help. But, Mademoiselle, please don't tell anyone. You don't know what danger – Madame Vagran is my aunt."

"Felicie, you may be saving my life. I would never betray you or your family."

Felicie turned as she reached the tower stairway. "And ... faith like your father's, Mademoiselle, if ... if that's what you've got, you'll win out, whether you get away from this place or not." She closed the door quietly.

Julie bolted the door and stood puzzling over these words. "Faith like my father's?" she repeated to herself. She had never connected faith with the Huguenots, but, of course, having a different faith is why they were hated. In claiming the Huguenots, she had simply named a group whose banner she would follow, an enemy of her enemies.

She moved back to the window and stared out at the murky skies. She rubbed the nape of her neck again as she looked at the river far below. When she realized what she was doing, she smiled. Philippe used to tease her about this habit. He accused her of "polishing her chestnut," and he nicknamed her "Little Chestnut." Her brown birthmark looked exactly like the shiny little nut.

In those days, she had worn her hair in loose braids, and the birthmark was visible. Now she was thankful that her hair hid the embarrassing mark.

For the first time, Julie wished her rooms were closer to the ground. Even if she could reach ground level, the marquis' men would be everywhere, guarding against her escape. It was like being surrounded by an army.

How would a person slip through an army? A spy would disguise herself as a beggar, merchant, or servant. Could she escape disguised as a servant girl?

She decided her best chance lay in leaving at night. But everyone would be carefully checked for messages and identity. In fact, chances were that no servant would be leaving. Could she pass for a man, as one of the marquis' soldiers?

Julie glanced down at the window seat where her cousin's cloak still lay. With a cry of inspiration, she flung it around her shoulders. It reached her hips. She cocked Albert's hat over one eye and posed in front of the big gold-framed mirror.

"Why, I could pass for Albert!" she told her likeness in the mirror. She wished he had left his breeches on the stairway, too, then giggled at the ridiculous thought. She felt excited and encouraged by her bold scheming.

Julie rummaged in her carved oak armoire but found nothing that resembled her cousin's riding breeches. She pulled out a dark blue silk skirt. Why not make a pair of temporary breeches out of this? She could buy a suitable dress as soon as she got away from here, because, luckily, she had saved a few coins from her last shopping excursion.

With scissors and thread, Julie worked on the slippery material all afternoon. It was hard work, and the garment looked odd. She hoped it would hold together until she reached that Huguenot farm.

Julie heard steps approaching her hall door. She hid her sewing and then opened her door to the heavy knocking. A uniformed stranger with a hard, cruel face stood there. A jagged purple scar divided his right cheek. His uniform colors confirmed that he was a sergeant in the marquis' escort guard.

The soldier insolently looked her over as he offered her a supper tray. He didn't speak. Julie took the tray and slammed the door shut, bolting the lock.

She wasn't hungry, but she uncovered the tray and found bread, cheese, and goat's milk. She drank the milk and removed the bread and cheese. These she would save to eat later. Without opening the door more than a slit, Julie slipped the tray through. She then locked the door. Before the steps receded, she heard a low, mocking chuckle.

Julie waited a few minutes before she brought her treasures out from hiding. She cut the last thread of her new trousers and tried them on. They were tighter than she had intended. As she looked them over in the mirror, she was glad her legs were long and slim.

She put on her red velvet jacket, then the cloak and hat.

"Hmmm, maybe in the darkness, but I'm not sure I'd pass in daylight," she mused. After all, she wasn't certain how long she would have to wear this costume.

Since she was to pose as Albert, she would leave when he normally left to go hunting. This meant she couldn't leave until early morning. She dared not sleep. She decided to use the time to improve her disguise.

Julie closed the shutters and lit her lamp. From the drawer of her wardrobe, she pulled a bolt of glistening white velvet, purchased to be sewn into a gown for Paris. Julie threw it on the bed and carefully unfolded and measured the velvet before cutting it into strips. While sewing, occasionally she would hold it against her chest and nod approvingly. Her fingers stung from needle thrusts caused by haste and inexperience.

Finally, she slipped into the new garment, which reached to her waist. It fit snugly, binding her chest tightly, hiding her femininity, and broadening her shoulders. She laughed softly at the vest she had fashioned. Her shoulders were now wide and padded. Julie had heard that most of the court gentlemen padded themselves to look more stylish and manly.

She tried on the rest of her costume and grinned with satisfaction. The only problem left was her hair. She pulled back the mass of brown hair into a braid and tried to secure it under her hat. But the hat perched unnaturally on her padded crown. Next she brushed it long and covered it with the cloak. That didn't work either. Julie was proud of her flowing, wavy hair. With sudden determination, she snatched up the hunting knife and hacked at her tresses. Long, jagged strands fell to the floor.

A strange lad looked back at Julie from the mirror. The uneven haircut left her hair curling in thick ringlets over her neck and ears. The lightness of her head made her feel giddy.

"Why, you look positively manly." she told herself, approvingly.

She chose a blue dress and a gray cloak from her wardrobe. These clothes she stuffed up the chimney to make her pursuers think she had left wearing them. Her cut hair was a problem. She hated to leave her hair behind, knowing that a sorcerer could use it to cast a spell against her. Nevertheless, Julie put out her lamp, opened her shutters and her window, and then stuffed her tresses into the thick brown and scarlet vines that covered the wall.

Julie nibbled on the cheese and bread, and gazed out the open window. There was no moon. A light rain fell. She decided to depend upon the servant Justine's young rooster to crow, giving her the signal she could leave. He always announced day long before anyone was ready to hear of night's end.

Julie put on knee-high stockings and wore no shoes. She would find riding boots at the bottom of the tower where they always were in wet weather. She put Albert's hunting knife into the cloak pocket.

Julie caught herself nodding. If she fell asleep, everything would be spoiled. But at last, she heard Justine's rooster. His solo crow grew into a chorus as others in the neighborhood joined his boisterous song.

She crept silently down the stairs. The darkness was overwhelming. She felt her way carefully past Albert's bedroom on the second floor. When she reached the bottom of the stairs, she knelt to feel for the boots. Just as she had expected, they were here. She planned to take her time and choose the boots that would fit her best. She hoped they would match.

The first boot was stiff and hard to move. She tugged.

"Ow!" she cried, flinging out her arms as rough hands threw her backwards in the tiny tower room. Her head struck the wall painfully. Before she could collect her dazed wits, a candle was lit, and old Justine stood towering over her. Justine was wearing the boots she had chosen!

Chapter IV
Escape

Before Julie could speak, Justine, full of apologies, helped her up. He was more frightened than she. In the dim candlelight, he mistook her for Albert just as she had hoped.

"Monsieur, young Monsieur! Please forgive me. How was I to know ye'd be going out to ride on a morn like this? Know ye not that guards are posted everywhere? If ye had used a light or told us ahead of time ..."

Julie rubbed her head, glad she had affixed her hat so tightly that it had only gone awry. Justine looked at her stocking feet and thrust Albert's boots at her. She would have preferred Francois' smaller ones.

Justine continued, "Your horse ain't ready, young master. I'll ..."

"No, no," Julie whispered, hoarsely. "I'll take care of my horse. You stay here."

"As ye say, sir, but I do think 'tis not the day for a ride."

Julie stepped into the courtyard, breathing a sigh of relief. If old Justine had been fooled – but she rejoiced too soon. A large figure loomed before her and demanded, "Who goes here?" He reached for her shoulder with a heavy hand, but she dodged aside. Justine rushed up.

"This be the young master of the house, that's who it be! You soldiers go back to your war, and let us take care of our people." He sounded full of resentment.

"What's he doing prowling around this time of night?" growled the soldier.

Old Justine answered, "Since when does a body have to get permission to move about his own property?"

Julie felt bolder. "It's morning, not night. I'm going for my horse."

The soldier made no more protests, and old Justine stopped Julie once more.

"Ye'll be wanting me to release the dogs." He started to shuffle away toward the dog pens.

The dogs! She would never get away with those hunting dogs loose. "No!" Julie called. Justine stopped, puzzled. She stammered a moment, then she said, in her lowest voice register, "I'm joining some friends, and we're using their dogs."

She moved toward the stables and waved Justine away. She was glad he didn't insist on following her. Albert's horse didn't want to obey her, while her own horse whinnied.

She saddled Albert's mare, swung herself into the saddle, and started down the lane. The guard who had almost ruined her escape opened the heavy iron gates for her departure. As she rode down the familiar road toward Orleans, the wind and rain swept away all traces of her drowsiness. Soon she could see dim light coming from the windows of the Vagran farmhouse.

As soon as she entered the farmyard, dogs descended on her from all directions, barking at her intrusion. She was glad she sat high upon the horse. Smoke rose from the chimney. "Who's there?" shouted a man framed in the open doorway.

"A friend. Please call off your dogs," answered Julie.

The man peered at her in the dim light of dawn. "Why, it's just a young lad," he exclaimed.

Julie dismounted as soon as he chased the dogs away. She heard cloth rip as she swung her leg over the horse. At least her trousers had gotten her out of her prison. She wrapped the cloak more tightly around her body.

"I'm on most urgent and secret business," she declared. "Felicie sent me."

The last words drove any remaining doubt from the farmer's rugged face. He turned immediately and motioned Julie to follow. The welcome odors of frying pork and an unrecognized hot beverage dominated the kitchen. The farm wife brought out an extra earthenware mug and plate as though it was common for a complete stranger to join them for early breakfast.

"Now, 'spose you tell us who you are, lad," urged the farmer. "I don't recall seeing you around here before, though I'm sure your horse is familiar."

"I am Julie de Mirovar, known as a de Beaulac at Valjean. I'm escaping from my uncle."

The man and wife exchanged shocked glances. "Mademoiselle de Beaulac!" exclaimed Farmer Vagran.

"Is it possible?" Madame stared in disbelief at this 'lad' who made such unbelievable claims.

Julie continued, "I was being forced into a marriage that I cannot accept. They won't let me return to my father, Jacques de Mirovar, Huguenot patriot of Aubusson. I must get to my father. If you're a sympathizer, I beg you to help me."

"We've heard much about you, young mistress, from Felicie and Ularie," said Monsieur Vagran, his eyes grave but revealing no dangerous commitments.

Julie stared from one face to the other. She pleaded, "Will you please help me with a different horse and a change of clothing? I can manage the rest."

The farmer paced the room, talking to no one in particular. "Can't have a young gentlewoman riding the countryside alone – country is infested with outlaws. The count'll be out to catch her, we can be sure of that."

"Sit down and eat your breakfast, husband. I'm sure we can plan better on full stomachs," his practical wife suggested.

Julie had already started to eat. She was surprised when the farmer, in a rich, expressive voice, began to pray. This brought back memories of her father, who had always offered a prayer of thanks before meals. She was touched and somehow strengthened by the simple prayer.

After eating silently for awhile, Monsieur Vagran spoke. "We sent Henri to the chateau yesterday with a message for Felicie, but he was chased away. Then Ularie came by and told us about the marquis. It's all over the village now, how you've angered the mighty monsieur."

He continued, "There's something else afoot. A young army fellow was out here early yesterday asking all sorts of questions about the count. He seemed especially interested in you and wanted to get a message to you. That's why we sent Henri to see Felicie, to get word to you for the young soldier."

Julie's heart skipped a beat. Albert had mentioned a soldier from her father's village. "Is the man from Aubusson?" she asked.

Vagran nodded. "That he is. Fellow named de Vauve."

"Philippe!" Julie whispered. "He has come to rescue me."

"Well, now, don't jump to conclusions," her host cautioned. "He didn't say anything like that. Fact is, he said he's leaving here today."

Julie's spirits drooped.

"The fellow seemed determined to get a message to you, but he lost interest when he saw how things were. Real young fellow to be a captain in the army. Who is he, anyhow?"

"Philippe is the youngest son of the late Count of Aubusson. I can hardly believe he's in the army. He always wanted to be a great scholar."

Monsieur Vagran jumped up from the table. "We can't sit talking all day," he rumbled. "Every minute counts. We've got to get moving."

Julie smiled happily, for this meant she would receive their help.

Young Henri appeared in the doorway rubbing his eyes, staring at the strange boy seated at his breakfast place.

"Henri, you eat later," his father said. "Run out and saddle Nester for me. Be quick."

Madame looked at Julie carefully. "This child has done such a good job on her disguise, don't you think she'll be safer to keep on passing for a boy? They'll be searching for a young woman."

"Oh, yes, I think I should be a boy, too," said Julie, patting the seat of her breeches under the cloak she had refused to remove. "But I simply must have some sturdier clothes."

Vagran grabbed his hat and said, as he rushed out the door, "Woman, fix her a lunch, and find her some clothes."

Julie quickly finished her hot drink. She wondered if this family risked so much for every Huguenot who came to their door. On the other hand, Vagran might be leaving to report her whereabouts at this moment. As she looked up to meet the woman's kind eyes, she felt reassured. She had to trust them. She followed her hostess upstairs.

"Nat, he's my son, left his work clothes here when he went off to the army," Madame Vagran said, as they entered an attic chamber. She found a blue serge peasant's smock and a white, much-patched shirt with long sleeves. Madame chuckled when Julie removed her cloak and revealed the improvised padding and the tear in her silk pants.

"Silk! Imagine that!" she laughed. She brought Julie a pair of brown homespun breeches. Julie protested when the woman gave her two wooden sabots to wear instead of her overlarge boots.

"Must I wear these wooden shoes?" Julie said.

"You'll be a sight wearing fine black boots with this outfit, my dear. The sabots aren't bad when you get used to them."

Julie tilted a soft woolen cap on her head and pranced about the room for Madame to examine. The woman clapped her hands. "You'll do nicely, young laddie. But what about a name for you?"

Julie hadn't thought of that. "Isn't your husband's name Joel? He's such a kind man for helping me. Yes, Joel. Joel ... Brunet!" She picked a last name out of the air.

"Perfect!" exclaimed Madame, obviously pleased.

They returned to the kitchen where Madame prepared a lunch of bread, cheese, three apples, and a slab of bacon. Madame shook her head vigorously when Julie offered her money for the food and clothing. When Madame turned her back, Julie dropped a silver coin into a shallow bowl.

Monsieur reappeared and outlined the plans quickly. The rain had stopped. "Ride my Nester as far as the blacksmith's place at the Red Bridge. Leave him tied there and walk as fast as you can the rest of the way to the city. Think you can cover three miles on foot?"

Julie nodded. "You must arrive in Orleans by eight o'clock. Go to the Inn of the Fox and ask directions to the house of Gaston the tinsmith, who lives nearby. Gaston is leaving with his family for Bourges. He'll take you along if you say I sent you. Of course, they don't know you're coming, so you must reach them before they start out."

"I know the inn – the blacksmith's, too," Julie assured him. "Thank you so much. Please don't worry. No matter what happens, I won't involve you in my escape."

As Julie mounted Nester, she reminded them, "Get rid of that clothing I was wearing, and the horse, too, for they belong to my cousin."

"No trace will be left of your visit. The horse will be discovered far from our place. If you miss the Gaston family, take the coach for Aubusson. Or go to the village of La Roche, where the Huguenots will hide you."

As she rode away, she was determined to reach the Gastons in time. She covered the road quickly on Nester. Soon she had tied the horse at the blacksmith's and started her trek to Orleans on foot.

The clumsy, clopping sabots were too slow to suit Julie. She sat down by the road and peeled off her wooden shoes and her stockings. She walked barefoot at a swift pace. But soon her side hurt, and her tender feet could bear no more of the road's sharp rocks. Not sure which was worse, Julie sat down and put the sabots back on her feet. The pain was almost unbearable.

"I have to go on, sore feet or not." she exclaimed aloud. She gritted her teeth and plodded on. When she was certain she couldn't take another step, she would pretend that she had only twenty more steps to go. She counted them off, twenty by twenty, and managed to reach the city gate.

Shopkeepers were opening their gray shutters. A group of girls passed Julie on their way to the water fountain in the square, jars balanced on their shoulders. She would have loved a soothing footbath, but she had to hurry on.

The innkeeper was outside opening his shutters when Julie dragged herself up to his place and asked for directions. He hardly noticed her as he rattled off the information without pausing in his work.

Julie forced her feet to follow his directions. She looked for the sign of the tinker. She leaned wearily against a wall and looked back over the way she had come. There was no sign of a pot and pan maker over any of the doorways.

A woman leaned out of her window to shake her bedclothes. "Where does the Gaston family live?" Julie asked.

The woman examined Julie curiously. "They lived right there across the street until 'bout an hour ago. I give 'em their breakfast myself, seeing they was leaving so early, and such a journey ahead." The woman would have kept on, but Julie stumbled back down the street. She fell, discouraged, beneath a tree and looked at her poor, swollen, bloody feet. She had never, never had such physical pain in her life.

She leaned her head on her knees and tried to think. She couldn't take a coach because that was the first place searchers would look for a runaway. Even a peasant boy traveling alone in a public carriage might draw more attention than she could risk. She should try to catch up with the Gastons, but the condition of her feet made that impossible.

A horse clattered by. Julie didn't look up until it stopped down the street. She couldn't hear the rider's question to the woman, still at her window, but her shrill answer caught her attention.

"You're the second one to come here asking for Gaston. What's going on? There's the other fellow, sitting under that tree." Julie cringed as the woman pointed to her.

The rider sat on his horse, thoughtful. He fingered a slip of white paper. Suddenly he wheeled his horse, guided him into a quick trot, and stopped before Julie.

She ducked her face downward and concentrated on nursing her aching feet. Was she being pursued already? She raised her eyes to look at the rider's puzzled face. Her heart took a sudden leap.

Philippe? It must surely, surely be Philippe! What is he doing here? The appearance of the uniformed young man who towered in the saddle awed Julie. He still had the same penetrating blue eyes, the same unruly dark hair that would not stay off his temples, and the same manner of drawing his brows into twin haystacks. But his mouth was firm, almost harsh. There were lines about his eyes that hadn't belonged to the boy she had known. The fun-loving youth Julie had remembered so fondly the past several years had been left far behind by this severe stranger.

He didn't speak at first; he simply stared at the slip of paper in his hand. His voice resonated in a deep bass as he said, "So you're looking for Gaston? Tell me, did you receive a mysterious message, too?"

Philippe was so intent on his message that he hardly noticed Julie.
Now as their eyes met, his eyes narrowed. "What is your name, boy?"
he demanded.

"J-J-Joel Brunet, Monsieur," she stammered, having difficulty
getting the false name out under his intent gaze that was so familiar,
yet so strange.

"Oh, it is, is it? Do you know about this note, then?" He jumped
off his horse and pulled her roughly to her feet.

Julie didn't have to pretend her confusion as she answered
truthfully, "No, no, M-Monsieur!"

"This note is signed 'J de B', and you've also been asking about the
man this note sent me to find. What are you up to? Speak."

She breathed a sigh of relief as she realized that the note had
agitated him, not recognition of her. She recollected her wits and
found she could enjoy this masquerade with her childhood pal.

"But, sir, my initials are not J. de B. You can see I'm just a plain
fellow with no claim to a nobleman's initials." She stuck out her lower
lip and looked at him accusingly.

"Or a noblewoman's." muttered Philippe to himself, but Julie
heard.

"Still," he went on, "you must admit it's a strange coincidence
that you are here with such initials. Do you know why I was to find
this man?"

"I do not, sir, but I know that I am lost, utterly lost, since I failed
to find him before he left for the south!" She crammed all the despair
she could into her voice, and into her face, as she sank back to the
ground. She lifted a swollen foot in her hands to massage gently.
Watching him out of the corner of her eyes, she added, "I simply must
reach Aubusson!" Philippe looked at her keenly. He then saw her bare
feet. His face showed genuine sympathy as he knelt to examine her

feet.

"Aubusson?" The word on his lips gave Julie a warm thrill, as did his hands upon her feet.

"Yes, I'm trying to reach relatives in Aubusson. My parents were killed last week," Julie lied smoothly.

"There is something remarkably familiar about you," mused Philippe. "Have you ever been to Aubusson?"

"Oh, yes, sir. I lived with my aunt's family for more than a year, but it was a long time ago."

"Who was your aunt?"

Julie had anticipated this question. Her quick mind had planned an answer. "Madame Irma, wife of Herbert Heron the blacksmith." He accepted her explanation without question. He puckered his lips and ran his tongue along their rim. Julie put her head on her drawn up knees and choked back a contrived sob. Then she looked up at him, wishing she could fill her eyes with tears, trying to look as helpless as possible. She began to pull on her bloody stockings.

"I'll just have to keep walking 'til I drop." She used the difficult Aubusson dialect. "If I could just find a gentleman who needed a boy, but ..."

Philippe threw back his handsome head and laughed heartily. "You little rascal! I'm still inclined to believe you're somehow connected with this note. Never mind, I'm going to Aubusson, too, but I suspect you've known it all along. Come, I'll put you on a stagecoach for Aubusson."

"Oh, no! Please, please, sir!" Julie had no intention of letting Philippe go. She hadn't decided how much she would trust him, but she did not intend to be put on a coach with dangerous strangers. "Please, let me go with you. I will cook for you, I will care for your horse – see, he likes me. I will ..." She stopped as Philippe regarded her suspiciously.

"My better judgment tells me I should either leave you here or put you on a coach. But for some mysterious reason, you fascinate me." He continued to study her silently while she squirmed uncomfortably. "You are what you are, and yet you aren't. Why should a peasant boy have such sore feet from walking?"

"But, sir, I've walked for several days, trying to reach the Gastons."

Suddenly his voice became severe and his grasp on her shoulder hurt. "Tell me the truth, are you running away from something – are you in trouble?"

Julie shook her head vigorously, looking at him with wide, innocent eyes. "If you're lying and I get in trouble over you ..." Philippe was still obviously undecided.

Now standing, she took a deep breath, threw back her shoulders, and declared, "Sir, I promise you on my honor that no one in all the world is looking for Joel Brunet!"

"Very well. First, we must buy you some shoes. Here, lead Chestnut for me."

"Chestnut?" she repeated as she limped after Philippe, leading the horse.

They found a cobbler's shop around the corner. When she had been fitted with shoes, which her tortured feet could not yet bear, he mounted his horse. "Come on," he ordered, offering her his hand.

She bounced onto the horse, behind Philippe. In so doing, she grabbed his left shoulder and wrenched it. He twisted with an outcry of pain and knocked her off the horse. She stared up at him, bewildered, from where she sprawled in the dust. She realized he was in pain.

Philippe recovered quickly. "Don't do that again, understand? Now get up here and be careful."

She couldn't persuade him to talk about his shoulder. He was quiet and sullen now. "A battle wound?" wondered Julie. "Maybe it's so bad that he can't fight anymore. Maybe the doctors can't cure it and he's going home to die." She found that these thoughts disturbed her more than her aching feet. She would be a good servant to him and take care of her "master" well. She would decide later when to confide in him.

As she pressed her cheek lightly against Philippe's broad back, she smiled. Her feelings, as they jogged along, were certainly not those of a servant-master relationship!

Chapter V
Road to Aubusson

The rain clouds had emptied themselves of their burden and were fading from the brightening skies. Occasionally, the sun flashed out to sparkle on the two riders who straddled Chestnut, riding south from Orleans.

Phillipe had rebuffed Julie each time she tried to draw him into conversation. She finally amused herself during their ride by watching for wildlife. She spotted one hare in a farmer's stripped field and a doe with her fawn almost hidden in green ferns just turning brown in the forest. She had just spotted her third deer rushing through fading pink heather when Phillipe guided Chestnut off the road onto a forest trail.

"I hear water," she remarked.

Philippe didn't answer. She could feel him swaying in the saddle but dared not support his sagging body. She had learned her lesson for that day.

Disregarding her sore feet, she slipped off the horse as soon as he stopped. Her feet sank into a cool carpet of dry leaves and velvety moss. She turned to offer assistance to Philippe. He brushed her aside. "Take Chestnut and tether him near the water," he said crossly, as he sank onto a mossy mound, closing his eyes.

When Julie returned, she took out the lunch Madame Vagran had given her that morning. "Here," she offered a share of it to Philippe. He hungrily accepted the food.

She glanced toward the horse, which also was munching a snack. "Chestnut is a strange name for a black horse," she commented.

"I've called all my horses Chestnut." He had a faraway look in his eyes. Little did he know that she remembered his first two "Chestnuts" almost as well as he did. She even knew why he had so named them. This secret made her smile mischievously to herself.

Philippe looked at Julie with a puzzled frown. "The more I'm around you, the more I sense a mystery. First you talk like an Aubusson street kid, then suddenly you're putting on airs with your talk. And I never saw a commoner eat so daintily."

"I'm a good mimic," she replied. "I think it's fun to observe all types of people and copy them." He didn't seem satisfied with her feeble excuse, and she resolved to concentrate upon acting her role more convincingly. She changed the subject.

"Why were you at Val ... uh, Orleans?" she caught herself. She had learned that her travel companion was a man of few words. She expected a short answer, but hoped that the relaxed environment might change his manner.

"It's a long story," he began. As he lay quietly looking up through the brilliant autumn leaves, he seemed to be withdrawing from her. When he did continue, it was as though she wasn't there.

"When I was a boy, I had a very good friend. My friend was happy, spirited, and loyal, I thought. We rode, studied, played, dreamed ..."

Julie sat still, hoping he would go on.

"My friend suddenly ran away. As a result, a person very dear to me was almost destroyed. I realized, with keen disappointment, that my friend was selfish and ambitious, like everyone else."

His voice became more bitter. "A few days ago I tried to see this so-called friend, but only because a great man begged me to make the effort. I stayed in a stinking inn in the country, unable to have my wound treated for three days. I went to much trouble trying to make contact with the party. Finally, late yesterday, this ... person sent a servant to tell me that Aubusson had never existed, that I was unwelcome, and that there was nothing to say to me or to anyone whom I might represent. So now I curse that ex-friend with all my power!"

It was fortunate that Philippe was so engrossed in his bitter reflections, because Julie had rocked back into the leaves, horrified and shocked. "That is not true!" she gulped, but he didn't hear. Her hands trembled as she pressed them to her mouth to keep from revealing her identity. She hadn't realized how completely her relatives had cut her off from her past. Knowing she must watch herself, she pretended an impersonal interest in this story. Carefully, she calmed her voice.

"Perhaps you've misjudged this friend. Perhaps she's a victim of circumstances."

Philippe struggled to sit up. He turned upon her, his eyes narrowed and cold. In slow, measured tones, he demanded, "Who said I was talking about a 'she'?"

A cold chill raced down Julie's spine. She wondered at her stupidity. Her mind fumbled for a story to cover this mistake, but it was unnecessary.

"Oh!" was only a soft moan as Philippe fell back upon the moss, his face white and taut.

She rushed to the spring and brought fresh water in the dipper that hung from Chestnut's saddle. She loosened his coat and opened his shirt. She gasped as she saw a blood-soaked bandage over his left shoulder and chest.

He recovered slowly. He didn't object to her efforts to remove the sodden bandage. She fought the dizziness that swept over her as she exposed the ugly wound. She remembered why his wound had been neglected, and this gave her new determination.

"Do you have fresh bandages?" Julie asked gently.

"No, I meant to get care in Orleans," he replied, his eyes closed.

She hesitated, biting her lower lip as she pondered a new problem. She rose from the ground and darted toward the birch thicket beyond the spring. When she returned a few moments later, she was no longer so broad in her shoulders. Philippe stared at the rumpled velvet cloth glistening in her hands.

"Where did you get that?"

"Why, it was hanging on a tree by the spring," Julie smiled, knowing that a ridiculous answer was as reasonable as a suitable explanation as to why a peasant lad should possess this elegant material.

She was intensely aware of Philippe's troubled eyes upon her as she cleansed and wrapped his wound. His manner changed from suspicion toward her to quick alertness.

"Listen, horses are coming. This is the only spring for miles around, so we'll have company. Hurry and cover that thing," demanded Philippe.

Six horsemen reined to a stop near them. She looked up into the repulsive face of the sergeant who had brought her last meal at Valjean. He was the leader of this detachment. Quickly, she bent back over her task.

The sergeant tossed his horse's reins to another soldier, who followed the others to the spring.

"Good day, sir," the sergeant saluted Philippe, whose officer's uniform would draw such respect.

Philippe returned his greeting from the ground and gestured toward his shoulder. The sergeant leaned forward.

"Hope it's not too bad, sir. You can't be on the same mission we are, after all, judging from that nasty wound."

"What mission, Sergeant?"

"Searching for the missing lady, sir." Philippe's lack of interest didn't discourage the sergeant. "Mademoiselle Julie de Beaulac of

Valjean disappeared this morning. She stole her cousin's horse and vanished."

"Why should Mademoiselle de Beaulac want to leave Valjean?" Philippe asked, suddenly interested.

"Aw, she's probably having a childish adventure," the sergeant grinned. "My commander, the Marquis de Feuillarde, is about to announce their marriage engagement. You know how some gals are when they are about to be brides." He laughed coarsely.

The sergeant didn't stop talking as he accepted a dipper of spring water from one of his men. "I don't envy the little lady when the marquis catches up with her," he said between gulps of cold water, "but I'd sure like to be the man who brings her in. I've seen that morsel and I liked what I saw."

Julie wished the intruders would leave. She hoped Philippe wouldn't notice her trembling hands as she worked gently and slowly. At last, the soldiers readjusted their saddles, finished watering the horses, and remounted. As they were leaving, the sergeant paused to say, "If you're traveling south, sir, I suggest you keep your eyes open for a fine, lone lady. It would be good for anybody's future to return this filly to the marquis. He's an important man and he's mighty anxious to get his girl back!"

Philippe sat like a frozen statue while Julie finished the bandage. He did not meet her eyes. She was uneasy, but she felt reassured that the sergeant did not mention her male disguise.

"Is that better, now, sir?" she asked, tying the last ends of the velvet bandage.

He did not answer. Julie felt pity mixed with alarm at the hate she saw stamped on his stone-hard face. She had no wish to be identified with the girl in his mind. Before he discovered her true identity, she was determined to prove that his false image of her was unjust.

The soldiers thundered onto the highway, and she started to rise from her completed task. She cried out as her legs were knocked from under her, and she landed, sprawled out, on the ground beside him. Roughly, mercilessly, his strong right hand grasped her hair and jerked her head against his knee. She fought furiously, trying to pull his hands away. She was no match for him, even wounded.

Philippe forced Julie's hands from where she squeezed them tightly against the chestnut mark on her neck. Then he thrust her violently from him and rose, trembling, to his feet. His eyes blazed with hatred.

"You! You! What tricks are you up to now? Why do you have to involve me in your escapades?"

In spite of his unfair attitude, she felt her heart go out to him. When she could explain, everything would be like it was years ago – or better.

"Don't look at me like that! I've lied only about my identity. I do want to return to Aubusson. Don't believe that dreadful sergeant, nor that false message you were given in my name."

Philippe's eyes narrowed. "You've improved upon the ways of deceit under your capable teachers at Valjean. Go back to them and leave me alone!" He started toward his horse but had to seize a tree to steady himself.

Julie ran around the tree to face him again. "Listen! You must listen to me. I hate Valjean. I've never stopped wanting to come back to Aubusson to my father. They would not let me. I've been like a prisoner in my uncle's home."

Philippe would not yield. His will showed none of the weakness his injured body revealed. "Don't try to fool me! I've heard about the fabulous marquis and his mysterious lady. That's popular gossip – how he brags of an exquisite woman he has in hiding, waiting only for the day of his choosing to reveal her to the court at Versailles! You! It's you!" Julie could hardly bear the contempt he showed in his voice.

"Wait, Philippe! What about my letters to my father – those spoke the truth!"

His contempt deepened, if that was possible. "Letters? You dare to speak of letters when your father grieved and yearned for one, just one little word from you?"

Julie's eyes brimmed with tears. "I did write, oh, I did write. My letters must not have gotten to him, just as his never reached me." She flung herself at Philippe, forgetting his wound.

"Philippe, please, please believe me," she sobbed. "I've wanted my father for all these years. Please don't keep me from going now."

He swung himself to the other side of the tree, but she followed, elated that her father loved and wanted her, but painfully aware that only with Philippe's help could she rejoin him.

"Shut up and let me think!" His harsh words restored Julie's hopes. She struggled to appear composed before him.

"Philippe, I've done a desperate deed in order to escape from Valjean and a man whom I despise. I would have escaped sooner, but I was waiting to hear that my father would welcome me. You must give me a chance," she paused, "for the sake of my father, if not for my own sake."

Philippe had eased himself back onto the ground. She could see that he was struggling with himself. She wondered why he was so bitter and unforgiving towards a confused child who had left Aubusson. Couldn't he see that it wasn't that child who stood before him now?

He stood up when he finally answered. "I'm still inclined to think you're using this masquerade for your own purposes. But for Jacques' sake, I won't expose you."

He pushed Julie away roughly as she started to grasp his hands to thank him. "It is for Jacques and Jacques only. Jacques is my friend – more than friend. He has been like a father to me, the only human since my own father's death who has ever been understanding. I saw his anguish when you and your mother deserted him. I saw his hope die and his loneliness increase when you wouldn't come home, when his letters returned unaccepted. I saw him ..." Philippe broke off. "No," he added almost to himself, "I'll save that."

Julie was so relieved that she didn't press the subject of Jacques. She would learn more about her father on the long ride south. She would ignore Philippe's resentment and win his forgiveness.

"By the way, I am Julie de Mirovar, not de Beaulac," she reminded him. "Or even Little Chestnut, if you remember."

Philippe whirled around. The fury was still in his eyes. "Will you drop all the calculating feminine wiles you learned at Valjean and remember that this trip is for Jacques' sake only?"

When Philippe and Julie continued their journey, they were no longer riding together on Chestnut. In spite of her objections, they took turns riding. Philippe declared that Chestnut shouldn't have to carry two burdens at once. Julie knew that this wasn't the real reason. Because of his wound and her feet, they traveled neither far nor fast. She kept scanning the horizon for a village where certainly they would get another horse. Then they would ride southward together, and Valjean would fade out of her life forever.

When they reached the Relais de la Poste, a stagecoach stop on the outskirts of St. Pierre, Julie was exhausted and hungry. It was mid-afternoon, a long time since the bread and cheese snack at the spring. Philippe guided his horse into the yard, dismounted, and gave the reins to her. After she led Chestnut to the stables to be fed, she started toward the front of the inn.

"Hey, you! Come git some chow." The rasping voice belonged to a stocky boy of about thirteen. She stopped, bewildered. "Your master ordered your lunch. Come git it," the boy repeated.

Of course, as Philippe's servant she would have to eat in the kitchen with other servants. She entered, ill at ease, remembering that she must watch their manners and copy them.

"You travel far?" asked the boy, who shoved her a bowl of soup and then sat down beside her.

"Orleans," replied Julie, carefully slurping her spicy, hot soup like everybody else.

"I work here. My name's George. You hear about that countess who sneaked off from her husband?"

"Not her husband," she corrected him, then wished she hadn't. "Her uncle, I was told."

"Well, I never saw such a fuss over anybody's niece," laughed the boy. "If you left from Orleans today, the soldiers will be stopping your master. They're stopping everybody. A while ago, they scattered a whole cartload of things belonging to a family moving from Orleans. I thought old Gaston was going to put up a fight, but he knew what was good for him."

The talkative George followed her outside when she finished eating. She approached the stable manager. "Did my master tell you we need another horse, one for me?"

The man shook his head, "Nope."

George laughed. "What makes you think your master is going to hire a horse just for you?"

"Just wait and see!" Julie was tired and impatient. Her lack of sleep was catching up with her.

When Philippe came out, she reminded him of the plan to get a second horse. Struggling up into the saddle, he replied sharply, "I've changed my mind."

George stood by with a smirk. "A man named Gaston is traveling south, sir, if you need a ride for your boy."

At the word Gaston, Philippe noticed George. "What are you talking about?" he demanded.

"A family from Orleans stopped at the blacksmith's this morning. They're going to Vierzon tonight, sir. There they are, that cart down there." George caught the coin Philippe flipped his way. He grinned at Julie, who ignored him.

"We need to travel faster than a loaded wagon, Philippe," she argued as she followed him toward the smithy's. "Saddle horses would put more miles between us and Valjean." She looked with apprehension at the tired-looking horse that was hitched to a very full wagon.

"You will call me 'sir' when you address me," Philippe spoke sternly. "A family is perfect. There will be less suspicion."

"And no chance to be alone with you," she thought with regret. Philippe stopped Chestnut and waited for Julie. "Before we see the Gastons, tell me what you know of the note I received this morning."

"I don't know. I've been thinking about it. The man who gave me clothes and a horse to escape may have sent it. He knew we were both from Aubusson. He may have guessed that you would follow those instructions if he used my Valjean initials."

Philippe rode on to where a family was climbing into the cart in front of the blacksmith shop. "Are you Gaston?" he asked.

"Yes, sire."

"Are you traveling to Bourges?"

"I am. We plan to arrive there tomorrow."

In a few words, Philippe had made arrangements to travel with them. "I shall make it worth your while."

Gaston's three small sons stared awe-struck at the tall soldier. On the improvised front seat, his wife sat holding a baby. At Philippe's command, Julie climbed into the crowded cart with them. The wagon was crammed with utensils, a broken cradle, several hard bundles, and squirming children.

Their scanty bedclothes were spread over this conglomeration. As the wagon lurched through the village, Julie decided all her soreness would merely be transferred from her feet to other portions of her anatomy.

The afternoon sun beat down upon the unprotected wagon. Julie was silent and aloof. Philippe rode several yards ahead. She didn't even have the pleasure of seeing him, antagonistic though he was.

She fought to control the growing giddiness inside her. Lack of sleep, the odor of the sweating bodies, the monotonous bumping of the wagon, and the haggling of the tired children made a miserable journey. When they handed moldy hunks of cheese to the children to quiet them, Julie jumped barefoot from the slow-moving cart and ran into the forest. She stayed near the road, but went far enough for bushes to shield her. After a minute, Philippe called, "Go get the boy."

The child peered around the bush and yelled, "He's sick, sir, awful, awful sick."

To Julie, that was an understatement. As her stomach retched miserably with her first experience of motion sickness, she wished they would all ride off and leave her in the cool quiet of the forest.

Chestnut broke through the tall ferns and she turned, embarrassed, to face Philippe. She didn't want him to see her like this: sick, disheveled, smelly, and dusty. Her misery didn't move him at all.

"Don't you realize we have fifteen miles to cover before sundown?"

"Do you think I'm pretending?" Julie stormed. "Surely, you don't think I enjoy this?"

"I believe you can control yourself if you realize the importance of avoiding delays," Philippe retorted. "Get out and walk when you feel ill."

"You can advise! You have a fine, fleet horse to ride. If you had to ride in that miserable, stinking cart with those dirty people, you might show a little sympathy."

Julie blushed beneath Philippe's smoldering gaze. "It's as I suspected. You've left your Aubusson heritage so far behind that you know nothing of life except the Valjean version. How ashamed your father will be of you!"

She regretted her hasty words, but Philippe was being unfair. She had fought all afternoon to keep her miserable stomach settled, her body from being punched and rattled to pieces, and now he thought that she was merely acting superior. She fumed inwardly, but her sickness vanished.

"Get back to that wagon and quit acting like a queen," he commanded. "These people are worth a dozen of your kind."

"You're ashamed of being an aristocrat," accused Julie.

Philippe turned too quickly at these words. "Sometimes I'm ashamed of what the high-born do, but I don't judge a man by his birth as you do. I realize people like Gaston haven't had the opportunity to learn cleanliness and manners. It's hard enough for them to keep food on their tables."

"That sad tale doesn't change one fact," she insisted. "They still stink and make me sick."

Philippe turned his horse abruptly and rode back to the road. Julie stumbled from the bushes and climbed sullenly into the wagon. She rubbed her sorest toe, the large one on the right foot. When she stretched her leg out, the rubbing continued. She resisted an impulse to jerk her foot from the grasp of the filthy little fingers of the five-year-old boy.

"I had a sore foot once," the child announced. "It hurt real bad for a long time, but it's well, now. Want to see?" Julie didn't, but he thrust his brown leg into her face anyway. She looked at a mangled little foot with two of the toes missing.

"Papa dropped a pan of melted tin on it," the child explained, matter-of-factly.

Julie drew her tired sore feet up and sat on them. She felt chastened. "Would you like to hear a story?"

The boy clapped his hands, and the two brothers turned eager attention toward her. The remaining miles slipped away faster as she repeated stories and fables that these children would never learn to read. Even the parents were silent, enjoying her stories as much as the children.

The sun had long disappeared when the church spires of Vierzon appeared in the distance, silhouetted against the darkening sky. Philippe rode ahead to make sleeping arrangements. Julie was so exhausted she moved almost in a stupor.

However, when they reached the Cavalier Inn where Philippe was waiting, Julie dragged herself from the cart to care for Chestnut. Philippe could easily have turned the horse over to the inn's stable boys. She believed he was determined to make the journey as difficult as possible for her.

Weary, she watered Chestnut and ordered his feed. As she left the stable, she noticed six tethered horses which looked familiar. She rubbed her neck, thoughtfully. She recognized them. The soldiers were at the inn.

Chapter VI
Traveling Companions

Julie entered the dining salon. A quick glance revealed that no soldiers were here. Philippe was already eating at a table near the fireplace.

Remembering her noon meal in the inn kitchen, she hesitated near the door, undecided. Philippe motioned to her. As she crossed the room to join him, she was glad she had thought to wash her face and smooth her hair. Philippe did not look up, however. He evidently planned to make her stand by and watch him devour spit-roasted pheasant, bread hot from the oven, and beef (or was it venison?) that retained a healthy red color. Julie drooled hungrily, knowing that cabbage soup would probably be her portion.

Philippe finally finished. "Monsieur." he called the fat innkeeper who waddled over to the table. "Give my boy here the same meal." Julie glowed. "He's been sick." His words mocked her as he strode toward the stairs leading to the guest chambers.

Julie was still eating when the six soldiers entered the room. The noisy men sat down at a table behind her. She listened carefully as their conversation turned to the lady who eluded them. She shifted her position to watch them from the corner of her eye.

The men, becoming rowdier in proportion to their wine consumption, made coarse jests about the missing lady. Embarrassed, Julie leaned over her food. Then she noticed that Philippe had reentered the room. He was scowling darkly as he walked to a seat near the fire and sat down.

"I say she's hiding somewhere near her uncle's castle," declared one soldier, as he waved his mug in the air. "After all, the horse was found less than a mile from Valjean."

"We even know what clothes she was wearing. We should have found her by now," another said.

"She could be in disguise," the first one suggested.

"We've been checking every woman, from little girls to grandmas," the sergeant said.

"Joel!" Philippe shouted angrily. Julie realized she had failed to recognize her new name, which he had repeatedly called out.

"Yes, sir!" she answered quickly, confused by the sudden attention focused upon her.

"You lazy, good-for-nothing clod! Do you plan to stuff yourself on my money all evening?" Julie ran to stand before him, blushing, wondering why his voice was so loud. "Do you want me to send you back to the North Country and let you live through that horror again? Have you forgotten how you whined and begged me to bring you away from the war, after I was wounded?" She finally caught on. She nodded.

"Get down and take off my boots," Philippe growled at her. The soldiers returned to their meal and to their conversation. She bent to do Philippe's bidding.

"Yeah, a man – that's possible. Or more likely a boy, like that kid right there," the sergeant said. Julie froze as she felt their eyes upon her.

A vicious kick from Philippe sent her sprawling on the floor, inches from the blazing fireplace. She leaped up, rubbing her stinging thigh and her singed elbow. Her anger was stronger at that moment than her fear. She glared back at Philippe.

The sergeant laughed as Philippe scolded, "I've had enough of your laziness and clumsiness for one day. Get out of my sight. Go find yourself a hole in the hayloft. If you know what's good for you, you had better work harder tomorrow!"

She started for the door, trembling from pain, anger, and weariness. "Kinda scrawny, too." observed another soldier, as she dashed out the door. She limped off to find the hayloft that she was supposed to share with the older Gaston children. She had to climb a high, narrow ladder that led up over the stables. The little boys were already asleep. She sank into a corner near an open window, rubbing her new bruises and thinking darkly of the man who had caused them.

Julie expected to fall asleep immediately, but the tickling straw felt like crawling spiders and the stench from the stables below stifled her. She envied the children who slept through the scurrying of rats, the flying of bats, and the frightening hoots of an owl who lived in the stables. Finally, overcome by sheer exhaustion, she slept.

When she opened her eyes the next morning, the hayloft was still in semi-darkness. The square patch of sky through the loft opening glowed softly with dawn colors. She sat upright, trying to recall why she should be frightened. Something had awakened her.

Voices below called loudly. Horses stamped their feet and jangled their harnesses. She recognized the voices of the soldiers and remembered why she wasn't in her own bed in Valjean.

She snuggled sleepily back into the prickly hay, relieved to hear the horses clattering out of the courtyard, the sound of their hoofs fading into the distance.

One eye popped open again as she remembered her duties as Philippe's servant. Her hip ached terribly, and her sleep hadn't been half long enough. But stronger than her desire for sleep was her determination to show Philippe that his opinion of her was all wrong. The children didn't stir as she crept to the opening and climbed down the steep ladder.

An hour later, Philippe stepped though the inn door and walked toward the stables. Julie didn't try to hide the sparkle of triumph in her eyes as he stopped abruptly and turned to face her where she stood by the hitching rail. Chestnut had been groomed, fed, and saddled.

He turned away to hide his confusion. "Is he ready?" He ducked his head toward Chestnut with a sidelong glance at Julie.

" Yes, monsieur," replied Julie, extremely serious.

Philippe turned to go back into the inn. "Well, I haven't eaten ... just came out to look at the weather."

"Liar! You were on your way to haul me out of sleep, to accuse me of laziness," she thought. She called to him, "I haven't had breakfast, either. They wouldn't feed me without your approval."

"I'll arrange it," he replied, not looking back. When he came out later, Julie was tying his parcel of personal effects onto the horse. The stiff leather thongs just below the saddle were giving her trouble.

"Let me do it," he said impatiently, close behind her.

"No," she said, working harder. When she succeeded in making it tight, she turned in mild triumph, surprised to find his face inches from hers. Caught off guard, Philippe couldn't avoid meeting her eyes. He stepped back quickly and turned to fondle Chestnut's mane, but not before Julie saw the pink flush of color flood beneath his sun-tanned skin.

She forgot the breathless wonder caused by this close encounter when he spoke again in that cold, impersonal tone. "I'm leaving you with the Gastons. I shall ride ahead and meet you somewhere later."

Before she could protest or question, he was in the saddle riding away from the inn. He did not look back. Her shoulders drooped as she sat down on a large stone. Did he really plan to meet her later, or would he do what he so obviously wanted to do, ride out of her life and forget her?

After eating the unexpectedly tasty breakfast that Philippe had ordered for her, Julie got up to help Gaston hitch the wagon. She cast her gaze down the road for some trace of Phillipe, but even the dust clouds had disappeared. Oh, Philippe, I wish I could hate you as you do me, she thought. She would not allow herself to believe that he was as hard and hateful as his actions indicated.

Anyway, she told herself, kicking a rock into the road and turning back to the stable, he had helped her slip past the soldiers, even suffering a setback with his wound. Then she remembered how vigorously he had insisted that he had not come to Valjean for her sake. What hold did her father have over this harsh yet tender young captain? What had the war done to him to make him so bitter?

"Where's the young captain?" asked Madame Gaston as she settled on the board seat in front.

"He rode on to Bourges where he will take a room and get some rest. He looked awfully weak to me," Gaston replied as he hustled the little boys into the back of the cart.

Julie was pleased to see that the Gaston's treasure, a fluffy feather comforter, had been spread on the wagon for her and the children. The ride wasn't at all carriage-like, but the knobby surface wasn't so painful now. Between stories and games with the children, she took several naps. With that sleep, along with rest for her feet and bruised hip, she felt more like herself.

Misty fog from the forest swirled about them during the early part of the day. At noon the sun burst through upon the unprotected cart. Julie had so many tender spots, accumulated in the last several hours, that she didn't welcome the idea of a sunburn, too. She borrowed one of Madame Gaston's baskets to wear on her head as a sunshade, and her little cart-mates laughed approvingly.

The magnificent twin spires of the Bourges cathedral appeared in the distance. Just north of the town gates, the oldest Gaston boy pointed toward a vast, round bowl of trees that stretched below and beyond the road. "Papa, is that where they have sacred meetings?" he asked.

"Hush! Hush!" both parents scolded him at once. As they swayed down the narrow, cobblestone streets, past the great cathedral, which reached endlessly into the sky straight above them, the boy whispered to Julie, "Look! No heads on the saints! The Huguenots shot them off. Papa told me." The child sounded triumphant and proud.

Julie looked up at the church, whose facade was rich with carvings, some of them, indeed, headless. "It's a beautiful, beautiful building, and I'm sorry that anyone wanted to harm it," she said solemnly.

The cart stopped in a dirt street so narrow that Julie expected the sides to scrape the dull gray walls of the closely joined shops and houses.

"Gaston, we've been expecting you," called a man from the doorway of a tiny market. "Wife, pour more water in the soup. The Gastons are here."

Other neighbors came out to greet them. The door to a dark, two-room apartment, the Gastons' new home, opened. Everyone helped the family unload the few things that they needed to set up housekeeping. Madame Gaston proudly directed the placement of the feather bed, the scant tableware, and the one bench on which she had been riding.

Julie remained with the Gastons that night. As she lay down upon the flat straw pallet which she shared with the three little boys, she wondered where Philippe was and if he would return tomorrow. She fell to sleep with the now familiar smell of straw enveloping her.

Julie awoke to the rattle of tin pans. The tinker wasted no time in setting up his business. Above the din, she heard voices. Her bedmates had risen and left. When she entered the other room, Madame Gaston offered her a cup of weak herbal tea and a hunk of fresh bread. She accepted it gratefully.

Monsieur Gaston assured her that Philippe knew the shop's location and would come when he was ready. She ate the rest of her bread by the doorway, watching anxiously for the uniformed rider. The stench from the street, which served as garbage dump and sewer, almost drove her back inside. As a well-bred young lady, she had been driven in bright coaches through similar city and town streets. She held a scented handkerchief daintily to her nose and stepped lightly across a carefully laid bridge walk when she needed to enter a shop from the carriage. If Aunt Isabelle could see her now! She shivered at the thought. Julie glanced with disgust at her grimy clothing and dust-covered skin. Her hair felt stringy and heavy with dirt. If only there was a fountain nearby where she could at least wash her face.

It was still early morning when Philippe, clean and rested, turned into the tiny street, leading another horse. Julie hid her delight at seeing both soldier and extra horse lest, out of pure meanness, he should let the horse go.

As they rode southward, Julie darted a glance now and then at her solemn, silent companion. She recalled with grim humor her dream of this ride with Philippe, how they would gallop along together on fleet horses. Except for the few times she was bold enough to attempt conversation, they covered the miles in absolute silence, broken only by the steady clatter of the horses' feet. When they stopped for lunch, he slept while Julie prepared their lunch over a campfire.

She repeatedly coaxed him to talk about Jacques, but he was more taciturn on this subject than any other. She finally decided that he refused to speak of Jacques because he guessed correctly that, above all else, she longed to talk about her father. It was more bearable not to broach the subject at all.

When they arrived at Montlucon, Philippe was welcomed at the Chateau du Moulin. A de Vauve son was an honored guest, meaning, Julie hoped, abundant food even for his servant.

She stood to one side, holding their horses, watching to see how Philippe would arrange for her overnight quarters. She knew he would want to report to Jacques that he had made proper and safe arrangements for his daughter in spite of her disguise. She had to admit that he had done just that (if a hayloft could be considered safe and proper) though he had certainly not considered her comfort.

"Of course, we have room for your boy, too," the host answered Philippe's question. "John, there, has an extra pallet in his room," and he motioned toward a tall, robust man disappearing through the kitchen doorway with a load of wood in his arms.

"That's very kind of you," returned Philippe, as Julie wondered uneasily if he had accepted this offer. "There's one thing I should tell you," he added, as though it were an afterthought, "I'm not sure, but there is a possibility that Joel was exposed to smallpox up north. In one village, we made an unfortunate choice of an inn and an even more unfortunate choice of a bedmate for Joel. Maybe there's no danger, but I'd be an ungrateful guest if I risked your household without a warning."

Julie saw the immediate reaction of all who heard these words. The host stammered, "Well, if you won't be offended, there is always the hay in the stable ..."

"Splendid, splendid!" Philippe was too enthusiastic in his acceptance. Was that a glimmer of humor she saw in his eyes as he turned to her? "Joel loves to sleep in haylofts, don't you, boy?"

She stared at him without flinching, making sure he saw no humility in her flashing eyes. His mention of the dreaded smallpox not only insured her a private bed in the hay, but it also guaranteed that no one would want to approach her with curious questions.

Julie didn't mind the hayloft that night. She was heartened by the thought that tomorrow would bring them to Aubusson – and home to her long lost father.

Chapter VII
Ambush

Philippe finally got away from Chateau de Moulin the next morning by promising to return soon for a longer visit. He thawed a little as they reached the familiar hills of the March Province, which rolled out before them like a lush green carpet speckled with the bright colors of autumn-bedecked growth. Julie inhaled the fragrant air, scented by the rose and violet blossoms of heather. Through delicate birch trees and clusters of dark junipers, she caught glimpses of a flashing brook.

She was sure that Philippe was not admiring heather and fir trees as he searched the forest on either side. She wondered if he worried about the marquis' men.

"Is something wrong?" She expected the usual rebuff, but today he was more communicative.

"My friends at du Moulin warned me that the renegade nobles have been making trouble in this neighborhood."

"What are you talking about?"

"Some landowners have refused to pay taxes to the king, so he has taken their estates, forcing them to become outlaws. They rob and plunder poor and rich alike. They are the terror of the countryside." Philippe maintained his wary, watchful manner as he spoke.

"Why aren't they stopped?" Julie knew the harsh government tolerated no rebellion of any kind.

"Eventually they will be, but our concern is for today."

She was glad that Philippe was finally talking. Riding mile after mile with a silent, hostile companion had been a strain. She had to choose her words carefully, lest she stir his memories and throw him back into his usual stern silence.

"What is our plan when we reach Aubusson?" she asked. "When can we stop the masquerade?"

Philippe puckered his brow in thought, but she guessed that he had every move planned. "We won't give up the disguise until we see Jacques and find out what the situation is in Aubusson."

"What do you mean?"

"You will soon see."

"You mean the religious situation?"

"Partly. Mostly."

"Are you Huguenot?" Julie asked abruptly.

"No!" he said sharply.

Philippe's answer surprised her. Why, then, had the Huguenot Gaston trusted him? Why had Joel Vagran entrusted her into his care? How could he have such love and respect for Jacques if he were an enemy of the religion Jacques placed above all other things?

As though reading her thoughts, Philippe added, "I'm nothing." This was a new thought to Julie. She thought everybody belonged to a religion, depending upon the family they were born into, unless they changed by choice. "Why are you nothing?" She was genuinely interested.

"I went to mass sporadically, enough to get by, until I went to war," he said. "I didn't want a military career. When my brother convinced me that it was the only future open to me, other than the priesthood, I went away determined to serve France well. I was lucky; I received a commission. In the war I discovered that instead of fighting enemies of our nation and king, I was pitted against my own countrymen – men, women, and children. In Strasbourg, I was a part of the so-called 'glorious victory' of our army, a victory based on starving a city full of free men who only wanted to practice a religion that someone with more power could not, and would not, understand." He seemed bitter as he remembered.

Philippe unburdened himself, forgetting his audience entirely. "Then we moved into the North Countries, Holland, for instance. Again we conducted a shameful war, with no provocation, upon innocent people. The magnificent Sun King himself came to add glamour and glory to the sorry spectacle."

Julie was afraid he had finished when he paused, sinking into reverie. She realized that some of his wounds were internal. Philippe was no soldier, certainly no party to the things he told about.

At last he continued, "In both places I found good people who became my friends. Later I saw some of them killed. I found one beloved friend, who reminded me of Jacques, starved to death in his sitting room in Strasbourg." Philippe reached into his pocket for a small black book. "I saved this book, which was clasped in his hands, because of his kindness to me, a lonely, confused young soldier, whose enmity he overlooked. I've read, here, the most amazing words."

"A Bible." Julie saw nothing so unusual in that. Jacques had always owned and read a Bible.

"Yes, but it was for this innocent-looking little book that my friend died. Another old friend lives for it." Julie wondered if he referred to her father.

"Then you are Huguenot," she said softly.

"No! I've seen Huguenots just as cruel and merciless toward Catholics as Catholics are toward them. How can people who supposedly follow the teachings I've been reading in this book be so evil and merciless to each other? Why won't men allow each other freedom to worship as they believe they should?"

"Jacques isn't cruel and merciless."

"Not usually, but ..." Was Philippe warning her? She remembered how Jacques reacted to her mother's Catholic preference, how violent his anger had been when he accidentally found a crucifix hidden in her cupboard.

Julie shook her head vigorously. "It's too much for me. I'll be Huguenot, since that's what Jacques will want."

Contempt shone again in Philippe's eyes as he glanced briefly at her. "You miss the whole idea. You can't take something like faith just because someone wants you to. I've tried and that doesn't satisfy. Nothing satisfies." he added bitterly.

Julie was encouraged by the unusual attention Philippe was paying her. She had finally broken through his defenses, his resentments. Drawing her horse closer to his, she pleaded, "Tell me how I can make up for my one childhood mistake of five years ago." Immediately she realized her mistake. His eyes filled with hate again.

"You needn't try turning fluttery eyelids on me, Mademoiselle de Beaulac. Your flirtations will have no effect upon me. You destroyed every decent feeling that I had for you years ago."

This unfair accusation angered Julie. Before she could protest, he went on. "I've avoided your company on this trip just as I've avoided my memories of you since your desertion of Jacques. I've seen you trying to practice your flirtations since I guessed your identity. If you expect to live undetected in Aubusson, you had better forget everything they taught you at Valjean and concentrate on being a plain, decent boy."

Julie remembered how she had tried so hard to adjust to the torturous journey, the smelly sleeping lofts, the unaccustomed labor. She knew she had complained very little and had fooled everyone except him into thinking she was a simple boy. She began to believe that Philippe had grown into an unfeeling, merciless man, too much influenced by the violence he had seen in the war.

"You're the most conceited, unfair person I've ever known!" she sputtered at him. "Because a little girl went away with her sick mother without saying goodbye, and because she was helpless to break out of bonds that even you couldn't pierce, you set yourself up as judge and condemn her. What do you know of tolerance and mercy?"

Philippe spurred his horse into a burst of speed and left her behind with her anger.

"Can't you stand hearing the truth?" she cried. He had disappeared around a curve. She spurred her horse to follow, but her horse failed to react as smoothly as Chestnut.

"Oh, you beast!" she turned her frustration upon the horse that had dumped her into the road, adding injury to her bruises and fuel to her temper. She scrambled to her feet. As her hand grasped the bridle, she stopped, listening intently.

"Thieves! Brigands!" Philippe shouted at the top of his voice, warning her. He was in trouble! Her first impulse was to rush to his side, but a loud voice stopped her. "He might be yelling to somebody. Go look down the road, quick!" the voice instructed.

She jerked her horse quickly into the thicket beside the road. She threw herself onto her stomach. Through the bracken, she saw a man come around the bend on foot, darting from tree to tree. He called, "Nobody in sight – I can see for nearly half a mile."

Julie watched him linger a moment, hoping her horse wouldn't neigh. The man turned and hurried out of sight, eager to join the plundering. She lay still, straining her ears to determine what was happening. Poor Philippe, being an army officer they might kill him! She forgot that only seconds before she had wished some catastrophe would fall on him.

What could a lone girl do against an undetermined number of desperadoes? Aubusson was only ten miles away, and she knew she could make it safely alone. However, she would be too late to fetch help for Philippe. He might be already beaten and dying this minute.

This thought jerked her to her feet.

She was startled by the neigh of a horse, which came from behind her. The lookout had been on foot. Perhaps they all were.

Julie tied her horse in the thicket. She slipped noiselessly through the trees, crawling through thick bushes, toward the sound of the neigh. She saw a clearing below, in a hollow, where a half dozen horses were grazing. A movement on the opposite side of the glen caught her attention. A stout, short man was struggling up the incline, making his way toward the noise on the road. She sized up the situation: the man was the lookout for the horses but wished to be in on the excitement on the road.

As soon as the man disappeared into the forest, Julie darted down the slope to the horses. She grasped their reins and joined them one to another. Then she led them back as she had come, out of the clearing, into the brush. She hurried the lead horse through the thick woods, disregarding the thorny branches that scratched her face and caught her hair.

Julie emerged from the woods not far below her horse. She released him, leading him quickly to the other horses. She had spotted a tin canteen and skillet tied to the lead horse. These she cut loose with the hunting knife she still carried. Leaping onto her own mount and grasping the reins of the bandits' horses, she urged her horse down the road toward Philippe at a full gallop.

"To the rescue," she shouted. "Save the captain! On you men! Forward!" She was banging the canteen and skillet together, hoping the noise would sound like clanging weaponry. Before she reached the bend that hid her from view, Julie turned the bewildered horses and galloped back over the ground she had covered. Again she turned the neighing horses in a fast circle and headed for the bend, still shouting, clanging, and galloping. This time she stormed around the curve, still pulling the horses. Her hands stung from the reins, and the frightened horses were hard to handle.

Just as she had hoped, the thieves scattered, leaving Philippe in the center of the road. He had been mauled and pulled from his horse. He staggered to his feet, his horse was still nearby. As he recognized her trick, his face brightened, and he struggled into his own saddle.

Two of the astonished thieves hesitated beneath the roadside trees, trying to determine if the band of soldiers was too formidable to risk an encounter. When they saw her trick, they threw themselves into the road, shouting and grabbing for reins. The horses rushed past, and Philippe kicked away a man who leaped for Chestnut.

Philippe caught up with Julie and reached over to take the reins of the bandits' horses. Without slowing down, she transferred the reins from her bloody hands.

"Is your shoulder all right?" she called out.

"I'm fine," he shouted, his eyes straight ahead. The stern, unyielding mask of indifference had returned to his face, and Julie remembered with renewed resentment his hateful words to her before the excitement.

She spoke to herself, softly, with no intention of his hearing her above the clattering hooves, "For a fact, Captain de Vauve, you aren't worth trying to win as a friend. Don't thank me for risking my life to save yours. Be haughty and unfeeling. I will soon be in my father's house, and I don't care if I ever see you again!"

Their horses followed the winding road around and over a steep hill. A lump rose in Julie's throat as the red roofs of Aubusson appeared below them. The Creuse River still snaked its way through the village, its silver band meeting those of other streams. The rugged rock peaks overhung the valley where the village nestled between hills. The ruined towers of the Aubusson castle rose like sentinels from an opposite hill. This was home.

She had imagined many homecoming scenes but never anything

this outrageous. As the tall soldier and the tousled boy rode through the town gate, people stopped to stare at the foaming horses and the strange riders. They stopped in the town square, where a crowd quickly gathered around the bloody officer with the slobbering horses. Julie scanned every face, hoping to see Jacques. The villagers were curious but suspicious. Then a craftsman recognized Philippe as the son of the former Count of Aubusson, and everyone's manner changed.

"Captain, the intendant is coming to hear your story," said a thin, tall man. Julie knew that the intendant was the man directly responsible to the king for the affairs of this province. Soon he came striding across the street, pompously self-conscious, his manner haughty and authoritative. Everyone, even an army officer like Philippe, was subject to the all-powerful intendants. It was partly because of these despised men (who had received civil powers formerly belonging to the nobles) that many of the noblemen had gone into outlawry or to Paris.

Julie stood back, rather dreading the attention she would receive when Philippe described the brilliant maneuver of his servant during their adventure. He answered the questions that the intendant, Monsieur Bregal, asked.

"There were six men in all. As you see, I escaped by dashing off with all the horses. If you send a party back immediately, you might catch them while they are afoot."

Julie rubbed the nape of her neck. The scoundrel! He was taking all the credit, with not one word about her part in the action. Where would he be right now had it not been for her?

Suddenly Philippe looked up and caught her eye. He smiled, speaking more to the crowd than to the intendant. "Of course, if you ask my boy Joel for his version, he'll tell you how he outmaneuvered six desperate outlaws single-handed."

The people laughed and looked at Julie. She glowered. Someone clapped her on her shoulder so hard, she crumpled to the ground, landing at Philippe's feet.

"Who's the little hero, Monsieur De Vauve?" asked the boy who had clapped her so hard. She recognized Auguste Craone, a boy near her age, whom she remembered well from childhood.

"He's a fellow who thinks he would rather weave tapestries than fight wars," Philippe replied. "Since I needed a boy on the road, I brought him along to Aubusson where I promised to find him an apprenticeship."

"How long will you be in Aubusson, Captain?" Monsieur Bregal resented Auguste's interruption.

"I've been released because of this shoulder wound, sir. Unless I am summoned, I'm not to report back until next spring."

The intendant nodded. Soldiers were often released during the winter months when it was impractical to wage wars. This relieved the army of providing for the upkeep of soldiers during this period, even when they were able-bodied, as this man obviously wasn't.

"You realize, of course, that during your stay here, when you're able, I will have duties for you," the intendant said.

"I'm at your service," replied Philippe. The intendant was apparently pleased by Philippe's respectful manner. Julie suspected that the resentful townspeople rarely extended the respect to him he felt was his due.

"Take care and get that wound healed," the intendant's tone was friendlier. "I'm glad to have an experienced officer in the village."

Monsieur Bregal went back to his building across the street. Someone set fresh apple cider before Philippe, and a huge hand thrust a mug into Julie's hands. She looked up into Auguste's coal black eyes.

"When will you tell your version of those heroic adventures?" he asked, a mocking grin on his broad, rugged face. "We like heroes much better than cowards."

She remembered that Auguste had always been a village bully. But she had been a spirited little girl who wouldn't tolerate his meanness. She recalled that one day during one of their frequent run-ins, she had gotten the best of Auguste. She made him trip over Philippe's dog into the water trough in the square. He was furious at first, but it was a turning point in their relationship. He stopped tormenting Julie and started respecting her.

But now Auguste was looking her up and down. "In this town don't be surprised if you have to prove how good a fighter you really are, especially if you want the reputation you claim."

Julie blushed as she remembered that Auguste liked to challenge new boys who came into town. "Surely he has outgrown that," she thought. Then, thinking of how embarrassed Auguste would be when he later found out he had challenged a lady to fight, she smiled at him. "Sure, anytime." He blinked in surprise.

Philippe stood up. "Joel, stay here and finish your cider while I go see about that job I promised you. I'm going to get you off my hands before I do anything else."

She dared not argue with him because of the crowd of people. But she didn't want to wait another minute to see Jacques, to find safety in Jacques' home. Full of resentment, she had to watch Philippe ride Chestnut out of the square.

"I don't see how he thinks he's going to find you a job." Auguste said. "You had any experience?"

"Not exactly."

"A lot of tapissiers have left Aubusson. The business is almost ruined. Maybe somebody will be desperate enough to take you on, but I doubt it." Auguste was trying to goad her, she decided.

She wasn't interested in Auguste or what he had to say. She knew where she was going, and it couldn't be too soon. As her eyes roamed across the square to the lively little river beyond, up the steep hill where a few brave cottages clung beneath the big rocks, Julie promised herself that never again would she leave her Aubusson.

In a surprisingly short time, Philippe reappeared. "Come on," he said, and they walked off together. He spoke low and fast. "I've told Jacques you're here. He has agreed with me that your masquerade must continue."

"Oh, no," Julie started to protest. Philippe motioned her into silence.

"The situation is desperate here. Dragoons are quartered in your father's house."

Chapter VIII
Jacques

Darkness descended quickly on the little valley town, especially in the narrow canyons that were streets. Dull gray dwellings rose like sheer cliffs on either side. Aubusson at twilight no longer seemed so lively and free. Julie ran a few steps to catch up with Philippe.

"Dragoons! Are they here after me?"

Philippe stopped in the middle of the public street. "Hush!" he frowned. He resumed walking, and she followed. She darted worried glances from side to side as they hurried toward the river. Obviously, word had raced through town that the young Monsieur, Le Capitain, was home. Julie noticed the faces that peered through cracked-open doors and half-shuttered windows, and the faces they met on the street. Some reflected good will, others resentment.

They reached the bridge spanning the river. Julie's brow was puckered, her teeth clenched as she realized that home, and danger, lay close ahead. Philippe stopped on the bridge. He looked both ways before speaking.

"These dragoons were living in your father's house before you left Valjean," he told her.

"Then why ...?" She stared at Philippe, bewildered.

"Have you never heard that horse soldiers are often quartered in the homes of Huguenots? They are given one order, to make life hard, as hard as possible for the heretic families with whom they live. Because of Jacques' influence upon the villagers, the intendant wants to make an example of him."

Philippe walked slowly over the bridge, Julie and Chestnut following. "You absolutely must realize the danger that surrounds you and many others, and watch carefully everything you say or do. Jacques thinks your disguise is necessary. He hopes it won't have to last long. He seems to feel that more than just your safety is at stake, so do be careful."

"Are the dragoons there right now?"

"No, we must get there before they return," and Philippe walked faster.

"Is Jacques glad I've come?"

"I suppose so."

"He's well?"

"He's ..." Julie held her breath to hear Philippe's answer. She shuddered with foreboding as he said, "he's different."

Has my father changed his feelings toward me as Philippe has? She wondered why she had never thought of this possibility before.

Philippe glanced sideways at Julie. Her apprehension must have shown, for he said, almost gently, "Jacques is anxious to see you, too."

The tall clock tower rose high above the town on a hill. The ruins of the chateau made a black silhouette against the darkening sky. Julie almost ran to keep up with Philippe as they reached the street at the edge of town that followed the sparkling river. The Way of the Tapisseriers looked exactly as it had five years before.

A lump was in her throat as they turned a corner and home lay before her. Memories, precious as jewels, tumbled around her brain as she followed Philippe through the gate. She wanted to cry out, "I'm home, Aubusson! I'm home!"

Their footsteps alerted the household, for the door was thrown open. Jacques stood in the dark doorway. Julie was dimly aware of faithful Lucienne in the background.

"Father!" Julie forgot all her fears and misgivings as her father's arms closed about her.

"Julie! Julie! Little Julie!" he was repeating in broken tones. "You've come home!"

Philippe reminded them in stern tones that sentiment must wait. "The soldiers may return any minute," he warned them. "We must make sure we tell the same story."

While Jacques' hand stroked Julie's face and hair lovingly, and Lucienne made little moaning noises about how that great big boy, girl, or whatever she was, had been the baby she had lulled to sleep many times, Philippe had trouble getting everyone's attention. Julie was eager to go into the kitchen whose light streamed through the door. She couldn't see her father's face, and she had waited so long for that moment.

"As we've already established," Philippe said, "this is an orphan boy I picked up in the north who wants to become a tapissier. His age is fourteen, his birthplace Brussels, and his personality cowardly and lazy." Julie bristled and Jacques objected.

"There are reasons for everything," Philippe said. "If she has a weak, cowardly reputation, she might avoid having to defend herself against the rougher citizens of our village." She now saw why Philippe had consistently bad-mouthed her. He remembered Auguste, too.

Jacques spoke. His voice was not as strong as she remembered, but it still carried authority. "What will we do if the dragoons refuse to let Julie stay? They've driven off all my helpers by their behavior, and they give no favors to Huguenots."

"That's possible, but I think I can take care of that." Philippe guided them quickly into the kitchen, for sounds of horses came from the courtyard. Julie still clung to her father as they entered the cozy room dominated by a huge fireplace.

She turned lovingly toward him, knowing he would be as eager to see his grown daughter as she was to see him. The daughter who had been a slight eleven-year-old child in his memory drew herself to her full, graceful height, and eagerly searched his face. Her happy smile dissolved into a grimace of terror. Her pained cry startled them all.

Lucienne stared accusingly at Philippe. "You mean you brought this child home without telling her that her father is blind?" Her eyes were angry, though tear-filled. Jacques was trembling.

Julie barely heard her. Her eyes, round with shock and unbelief, were drawn as though hypnotized to the horrible, scarred face with sunken, unseeing eyes – the disfigured kind of face that usually stared from beggars' rags, a discolored, peeled face like those she always avoided looking upon.

Philippe's discomfort showed in spite of his brusque manner. "Just make sure she knows how it happened. They're coming!" he whispered fiercely. "Pull yourselves together."

But Julie was unaware of anything except this tragedy. Her brave, strong father was a wasted frame with no face. The sanctuary-home she had yearned for was more dangerous than Valjean. Of all the mean things Philippe had done to her, surely this was the lowest. She sobbed uncontrollably, her voice rising with each sob. Philippe glanced desperately at the door through which the soldiers would come.

"Stop it!" He slapped her hard on the cheek. As the door burst open, Julie was staring defiantly at Philippe, her face tear-stained but controlled. Jacques, who heard the slap, stopped his motion toward Julie's defense just in time.

"What goes on here?" the surprised corporal demanded. Two more dragoons crowded to peer over his shoulders.

Philippe turned with a shrug. "Just a problem with my unruly servant. I am Captain de Vauve of the King's Blue Cavalry. I've returned to Aubusson to recover from a battle wound."

The corporal saluted clumsily, flustered by the unexpected

encounter with an officer from the famous Blue Cavalry. "Corporal Lafayere, sir," he said.

"I brought this lad home with me, hoping to find him a place in a tapisserie. I no longer need his services. I didn't realize that this house is entertaining dragoons." The corporal grinned at this subtle reference to their quartering. "I had thought Jacques might teach the lad his trade, for everyone says his skill is still remarkable despite his blindness."

"So they say." The corporal would want to please this pleasant captain, but he hesitated to let Jacques have an apprentice.

"Does the old man want the boy?" he asked.

Before Jacques could answer, Philippe said, "Of course not!"

"Is that so?" The corporal relaxed a little.

"May I speak to you privately outside?" Philippe said. The other two dragoons made themselves at home by the fireside. Philippe beckoned to Julie to join him and the corporal outside.

"I'm sure I can find another place for the boy, if you prefer. He's sneaky as an eel, but seems to have real talent for weaving. He's loyal enough to me, but watch out if he isn't on your side." Julie saw him wink again at the corporal.

The corporal scratched his head. "We got ourselves a tricky deal here. There's something going on in this town, and, try as we do, we can't uncover it. We think this old man is still the brains and leader behind the Huguenots. Far as we can tell, all church meetings have stopped, and we've stamped out the movement, but still ..."

Philippe appeared impressed. The corporal stroked his tangled beard as he spoke. "Do you reckon this boy could sort of spy on the old man for us? These tapissiers are disappearing so fast it's getting hard to turn out enough tapestries to please the king. The intendant is getting rough on us. One morning the people are here, the next they're gone."

"Wonderful! Your plan is just the answer." Philippe's words made the corporal swell with pride. "Why don't you try it? Old Jacques used to be a friend of mine. I'll fix it so he won't suspect a thing."

"Yeah, I just know he's the one to blame for a lot of our troubles, but not for long."

Julie stiffened. Philippe said, "Why don't you make the boy sleep in his bedroom with him?"

"Hah, the old man got no bedroom – it's mine! But the boy can sleep in the weaving room where we got the old man sleeping. Sure."

The two men faced Julie with grim faces. "Do you understand what you're expected to do?" asked Philippe.

"Yes, sir!"

"You gonna report direct to me, understand?" growled the corporal.

"Yes, sir!"

"If you mess this plan up, I'll turn you in as an army deserter, and you will never become a tapissier!" Philippe threatened.

"I promise I'll do whatever you say, sir."

"You concentrate on being a loyal French citizen under the king, for the present, and maybe you can pick up some weaving tips from this old master while you're at it." Philippe turned to mount Chestnut. The corporal opened the gate for him and saluted as he rode away.

Julie reentered the cottage behind Lafayere and vaguely heard him declare that the boy was to become part of the household. She was exhausted from her long, hard trip, and the cruel shock of her homecoming had almost undone her. She swayed from weariness, and Lucienne looked at her anxiously.

"Best the lad be sent to bed, or he's going to collapse all over the kitchen." the woman said.

Julie followed her to a cot in the big tapestry room across the hall from the kitchen. "There, you can take the master's cot, and we'll fix him another place," she said gently. "Poor, poor baby."

What a way to come home." She touched Julie's rough, sore hands and caressed her tangled hair. Julie tumbled into bed and barely felt gentle hands remove her boots before she dropped into a deep sleep.

When she first opened her eyes the next morning, she seemed to have slipped back into her childhood, for she could hear the occasional click of a shuttle at the tapestry loom and the muffled roar of the little river outside. She could see the bent figure of her father half sitting on the thick wooden rod that was the bench for the table-like loom. She watched his skillful movements, his weaving little slowed by his handicap. "How does he do it?" she wondered with pride.

Waves of love and compassion rolled over Julie. A tear slipped from her eye as she watched his face, no longer the merry face she remembered. His stooped frame and wasted hands further revealed the hardships he must have endured.

"Are you awake, Julie?" The question was so soft she thought at first she had imagined it.

"Yes, Father, how did you know?"

"When we lose one gift, God gives another to take its place," he answered. "I felt you awake."

"How can you speak kindly of a God who took your family, your prosperity, your eyes – everything from you?" she asked.

"Hush, Julie. You don't know what you're saying. God is good to me. Don't you see He has brought you home to me just in time?"

"In time for what?" she tried to wipe the bitterness out of her voice.

"You'll see, my dear. In the meantime, he has kept you safe from what you would have suffered here as my daughter. He was wiser than I, who wanted you sooner."

Julie swung her legs over the edge of the cot and sat up. "But I should have been here with you, and I would have, Father, if I could have come."

Jacques' gentle voice calmed her. "I've never doubted you, Julie. But now I see that it was best for you to be away."

"It was not best!" she argued. "I've wasted five years of my life while you were needing me. Now, I shall never leave you and Aubusson again."

"You see, Julie, God is working in our lives just as I work this tapestry. Under His direction, if we cooperate, the tapestry becomes a masterpiece."

"Father, tell me how you became blind."

Jacques sighed. "I don't think you need to know, but someone will tell you if I don't. You must promise not to be bitter. Bitterness and hate fester like a wound that won't heal. It's dangerous to hold those feelings within one's soul." Julie thought of Philippe.

"When I learned of your mother's death, several months after she died, I made a trip to Valjean to bring you home. Since Philippe had been summoned to Paris to receive an army commission, we traveled together. When we reached Valjean, Claude refused to see me or allow me to enter the estate. I feared he kept you, not out of love, but as a means to his private ambitions."

"I made a nuisance of myself with my threats and speeches in the village. One evening as I was returning to our inn, a man leaped into my path and hurled something into my face. It was a burning chemical. It's a miracle I didn't die, a miracle and Philippe's care."

"Oh, no!" She smothered her weeping, lest he stop.

"Philippe took me to Orleans to the best doctor he could find. He risked losing his commission to bring me safely back to Aubusson, or I wouldn't have made it. But Philippe …" Jacques shook his head sadly. "Philippe was more seriously injured than I. His anger is not directed only at you, Julie. We must be patient with him."

The puzzling facts started to jell in Julie's mind. Philippe's hate towards her and his excessive concern for Jacques made a little sense. "But you're not bitter." she marveled.

"I can still weave. I can tell darkness from light. I have many friends. I now have you with me, in answer to my prayers."

"How can you possibly weave, Father?"

"I don't need eyesight to weave, Julie. My only problem was the colors. Lucienne has learned to arrange the colored wool that I need just as I instruct her."

"And I'm sure you're still the best weaver in France!" declared Julie. "I slept late, didn't I?"

"Yes. The soldiers left early to search for the outlaws you met yesterday. Life will be hard for you here, Julie, but we shall bring an end to it as soon as possible."

"What do you mean, Father. Can you make the soldiers leave?"

"No, no. I hate this masquerade more than you know. But you're in great danger. Men of the marquis were here yesterday to question us. The intendant resented their interference here, for he needs the soldiers in this area to control the outlaw nobles and the Huguenot exodus. He has enough problems without searching for a missing woman."

Julie hadn't realized her father knew about the marquis. "Do you think I can get by with my disguise in Aubusson?"

"You must! We can trust no one. There are spies planted even among friends."

"Oh, do you know I am a spy to watch you?"

"I suspected as much," he smiled. "I'll tell you what to say to the soldiers. Under no circumstances are you to tell them anything else, and you must always obey any commands I give you immediately. Will you remember?"

Julie noted his sudden earnestness. She recalled the dragoon's declaration that something was going on in Aubusson. Was her blind father really involved in this mystery?

Lucienne interrupted. "This child hasn't had a morsel of food since she got home. Now, come into the kitchen and eat!"

Lucienne placed two tiny roasted fowls on the table before her. "Lucie! You're still the best cook in France," she mumbled between bites. "No wonder the dragoons are quartered here. They know where to find the best eating!"

"Huh!" Lucienne was pleased. "That's not for the dragoons. They get soup, soup. Meat only when they furnish it. You notice they've cleaned out our chicken and pigpens? The robbers!"

"How do you manage?"

"We manage because the master's got so many loyal friends, that's how. Folks sneak parcels of food to me, or he would have starved long ago. They don't care if he don't eat."

"Isn't it risky for people to bring food here?"

"Of course it is. But the master is our shepherd, the shepherd of Aubusson. There are enemies, too, mind you, but we do our best to protect your father." Julie looked up at Lucienne, puzzled. "We lost our pastor three years ago. He disappeared, and the intendant won't allow another pastor to come. So everybody looks to your father as the shepherd."

"Even though he's blind, he is their leader!" exclaimed Julie.

When she was through eating, she returned to the tapestry room to work with her father. He showed her which loom to work on, and she seated herself on the hard bar. She remembered how this room was once filled with happy workers, all skillful weavers under the direction of Jacques. Even when her father was busy supervising and directing much of the work done in Aubusson, he still found time to work on his own weavings.

"I think I'll learn easily, Father. The music of the looms is a part of me," she said, as she accepted the simple rolled up design that he assigned to her. Carefully she placed it beneath the cotton warp on the loom. She could see the unrolled top portions of the design only, and the colors were indicated on the designed cartoon.

"The best work is already done," she complained. "The designer gets to choose the colors and plan the work. The weaver only follows the directions."

"But the weaver must follow the design precisely," said Jacques. "Aubusson designs, worked in rich colors, are what make the tapestries of our village so sought after."

"Do you still design?"

"No, I can no longer create the cartoons, but I weave those I remember. Other weavers in the village still use my old cartoons. They prefer them over the designs of the new artists who only know how to paint and draw, not weave."

Julie remembered how popular her father's tapestries had been as practical furnishings for the chateaux and city estates for the aristocracy and merchant classes. Tapestries were not only decorations but served as essential partitions to stop cold drafts and as movable walls to divide large rooms. Now that the king kept his nobles in Paris, tapestries were becoming more of a luxury, serving as decoration almost entirely.

"Lafayere will question you about your afternoon's work," said Jacques after they had worked side by side for some while.

"What shall I say?" she asked, as she paused in her work.

"Tell him I refused to discuss anything with you, that I questioned you instead. Tell him I was particularly careful to avoid a discussion of religion."

"Why say you avoided religion, Father, when that's what he wants. Tell me something safe about it."

"Religion is the most dangerous topic in Aubusson at the moment,

Julie, and you must remember that when you're in the village. I don't know how much of your Huguenot heritage you've retained, but you must hide all your reactions to religious questions and to any persecution you might see in town."

She put her shuttle down. "Father, I have heard even in Valjean that you're in danger. It seems strange that a blind man should be so feared and threatened."

"Our strength is spiritual, not physical. Our enemies are beginning to realize this, and they have no weapons to use against a victorious spirit. Some of our people have given up under persecution, but not many. Ah, Julie! If you could know the great, unquenchable souls I have known!"

She wondered how powerless, hunted Huguenots could be considered victorious. Though beyond her understanding, she sensed something of what he was trying to say in his own unyielding courage. She resumed weaving.

Darkness crept stealthily into the shadowy room. Julie could hardly see her cartoon when Lucienne entered with a candle. She stared, perplexed, as Lucienne walked to the unshuttered window and placed the lighted candle there. "I need the light over here, Lucie. I can't see what I'm doing," she said.

"No, the candle is sufficient. You've worked enough for today." Jacques never paused in his click, clack of the loom.

"But I shall bring the light over here where it will do some good," insisted Julie, as she rose and started for the window.

"No!" The stern command of her father startled her. She wondered why a candle should be wasted across the room, but decided her questions would be unwelcome. She went back to her loom, gathered the unused wool threads, and returned them to the skein holder.

"You see, sometimes the loss of sight is no handicap at all," said

Jacques, working on in the twilight. He was seated so that he faced the lighted window. His back was bent, but he showed no signs of the fatigue that plagued Julie.

"Father, do you work so hard all the time? You really should spare a few minutes to rest."

"A darker night than this is coming, Julie. I must use every minute I can."

Julie forgot the questions she still wanted to ask. Her father's face lifted expectantly, and she glanced at the window just in time to see the candle go out. The sky through the window was not yet black, but the room was quite dark.

"Go! Go quickly to the kitchen and don't come back until my door is ajar." Jacques spoke so urgently that she immediately hurried away. She heard the bolt thrown a few seconds after she closed the door.

What made the candle curiously go out, and why had Jacques reacted so strangely? Whatever it was, Julie was sure that Jacques would handle it. She hoped he wasn't exposing himself to more danger.

Chapter IX
Under Suspicion

The steamy kitchen was pungent with the smell of cabbage soup. Copper pans hanging from the ceiling sparkled in the glow of the fire. Lucienne, who was bending over the soup kettle in the fireplace, turned with a mild scowl when she heard Julie dump short logs into the wood box. "That's my job," she scolded.

Julie smiled at her. "Are you trying to spoil the boy-apprentice?" Then she whispered, "Lucie, there is twice as much wood in the woodpile as there was this morning, and a basket with eggs and bread is hidden there."

Lucienne placed her hands on her stout hips, and her broad, red face beamed. "Sure, sure, there would be when the food in here is all gone." She bobbed her head up and down, then stopped still. Julie heard the horses outside, too.

"The soldiers!" she whispered, thinking of Jacques' danger if he was caught in a suspicious situation. She was almost certain that Jacques had sent her away in order to receive a visitor through the window. Lucienne, however, displayed no anxiety, and she turned back to her soup kettle.

Racing out into the darkness, Julie took the dragoons' horses. She tried to delay the men with conversation, but they were hungry and impatient.

"Shut up and unsaddle the horses," Lafayere said. He stomped into the house with Lucas and Gautier, his two companions.

She finished her job as quickly as she could. On her way back to the kitchen, she saw that Jacques' door was no longer ajar. No sound came through the closed door.

Lafayere unbuckled his sword and handed it, along with his musket, to Julie. She stacked them in the corner and returned to take the weapons from the other two dragoons.

"Bah! Cabbage soup again," complained Gautier, forcing his fat frame onto the bench before the rough oak table. Four earthenware bowls were on the table. Julie took her place with the men, and Lucienne filled the bowls. Tin cups held wine from the soldiers' wine supply, but Julie's contained a hot drink flavored with herbs. When Lucienne passed out the bread, she tried to give Julie a larger share, but Lucas objected.

"Don't you see how that woman favors the boy? Waits on him like he's better'n us. I told you something's wrong."

"Naw, the old woman is a frustrated hen with no chicks," Lafayere shrugged. "The boy's been buttering her up in hopes of extra rations, I guess. And I can stop that."

"I don't like him, I tell you," Lucas persisted. "He puts on airs like he was gentry. Look how he eats, how he talks."

These words startled Julie. She thought her careful mimicry of the soldiers' behavior had been convincing.

Lafayere kept right on eating. "Seems Lucas, here, thinks we oughtn't to trust you, Joel," he said, between huge bites of hard, dark bread. Julie decided silence was the safest response.

Lucas scowled. "He could be a Huguenot spying on us, for all we know."

Lafayere stood up abruptly. Leaning across the table, he grabbed the front of her smock. She looked up into his threatening eyes.

"I think you got more sense than that, but you better not ever try to double-cross me!"

Julie didn't have to pretend alarm. "I'm too smart to join up with the losing side, Corporal. You should know that."

Releasing her slowly, Lafayere walked over to light his pipe from the fireplace. "What did you learn today?" he asked her.

"Well, seems like Lucas isn't the only one suspicious of me. The old man talked free enough but only to ask me questions. Seemed to want to know all about me, but wouldn't talk about himself."

"That's good, that's a good sign. He's got to know you before he can trust you," Lafayere said. "Maybe he'll try to make you help him do whatever rotten business he's up to." Smoke puffed vigorously out of his pipe, and he looked confident of success.

"What makes you hold off if you think he's such a leader?" Julie asked, more interested in the answer than she dared show.

"We got to know the whole picture. After all, he's blind, and so he can't do much all by himself. One thing you got to help us find out, who's helping?"

Lucas spoke, "Let's have another inquisition. Let's see if he'll answer our questions this time."

"Gautier, get him."

Gautier, who had been dozing, grumbled, "Let Joel."

She couldn't see her father's door to tell if it was still closed. She must not let Jacques be disturbed at any cost.

"No! He's tired, why bother him?" She realized her mistake immediately as suspicion flared again from Lucas. He got up so quickly, the bench overturned. He struck at Julie savagely but barely grazed her cheek. She followed as he dashed across the hall and flung open the door of the tapestry room. Peering fearfully past Lucas, she saw her father still bent over the loom in the darkness, just as she had left him.

"Is the day done, truly?" came his gentle voice. "Please forgive me if I've kept you waiting." He got up slowly and started toward them, halting, feeling his way.

Lucas stared blankly at the innocent old man. He suddenly lost interest, flinging himself toward the outside door and into the yard. Julie lingered just inside the room, her eyes searching the darkness for some clue to the room's mystery. Far off toward the woods behind the house, she heard a horse neigh. Dogs barked in the distance. A shiver of expectation raced down her spine as she wondered what part she would have to play in the intrigue surrounding her father.

Jacques woke Julie early next morning. Lucas and Gautier had left earlier, but the corporal was still in his room. While they ate a quick breakfast of eggs and bread in Jacques' room, father and daughter talked softly.

"I want you to be away before Lafayere awakes," he told her, after she had told him of Lucas' suspicions and hostility. "The less these men see of you, the safer you will be." He went on. "I need wool from the village. Do you remember where the Lafaud Wool Shop is?"

"You mean Jeanne's house? Yes. What has become of that too fancy little girl who never got along with me?"

"She's a fine young woman. Jeanne and her family are dear, dear friends. As children, you two were too different to get along well. Jeanne resented your exhausting energy and you resented her softness," Jacques smiled.

With a basket swinging from her hand, Julie set out for the market square where she would find the shop. It was market day. The narrow streets were crowded with carts and people.

Julie heard a loud commotion beyond the square. Several persons were coming toward her, ducking into doorways and side alleys. Others hurried toward the noise with expectant faces. One little boy kept yelling, "Dog! Dog! Dead dog!"

Julie had almost reached the shop when the crowd swirled apart to make room for Lucas and Gautier. Lucas was clearing the way for the burden that Gautier's horse was pulling through the slimy streets.

Julie stopped, horrified by the sight before her. The burden was the body of an extremely old man, most of his tattered garments pulled from his body. Bare bones showed where the sharp stones had cut away skin and flesh. The body was covered with the filth of the streets, exposed to the jeering, curious crowd.

Julie leaned against the wall. She turned her back on the revolting scene, stumbling down the street, supporting herself by clinging to the walls of the shops and houses.

She passed under skeins of wool hanging over the doorway into the Lafaud shop. She leaned against the closed door, trembling, trying to regain her composure. A gentle voice made her open her eyes.

"Have you never seen a Huguenot funeral before?" There was only a trace of bitterness in the young voice, and the soft blue eyes were kind.

Julie struggled to speak. "A Huguenot? You mean, that's all? Not a thief, or ... or murderer, just a Huguenot?"

The crown of soft brown hair shook slowly. The girl's face wasn't beautiful, but her expression was kind and lovable. It was Jeanne grown up.

Julie tried to banish the dreadful thought that tormented her, that brought tears to her eyes. That could be Jacques!

"Who was he?"

"Old Dominique. He was a Huguenot a long time ago, then accepted a government bribe to change his religion to Catholic. He became sick and yesterday, when he was dying, he refused the last sacraments of the Church. He screamed out defiance against the priest. The intendant decided to make an example of him. Dr. Boulard stopped by this morning and told us about it."

"What will they do with him now?"

"Throw his body outside the village and dare anyone to touch it, to bury it. I'm sure you've seen things worse than this. Aren't you the lad who came here with Monsieur Philippe?"

"Yes, I'm Joel."

Jeanne's blue eyes widened. "Oh, yes, I remember. You didn't like the war. Well, I don't blame you. I couldn't bear that sort of life, either, or that ..." as she flung her hand toward the street where the normal day's bargaining over farm products was replacing the noise of the jeering mob.

"Tell me about Monsieur Philippe. Is he hurt very badly?" There was unusual fervor in the question.

"He'll recover."

"Do you think he will remain in Aubusson?"

"He tells me very little of his business," retorted Julie, resentful that she should mind Jeanne's questioning about Philippe.

"Why don't you two get along?" Jeanne was laughing now. "For a pair who traveled across a country together, it seems you would have developed a little companionship."

"He's too stubborn and rude to be a companion," Julie said.

"He is not! He's a wonderful gentleman. You're a fine one to be talking about rudeness." Jeanne's face flushed.

"Monsieur Mirovar wants some wool, the usual quality, undyed. He needs at least ten skeins immediately," Julie recited the order precisely.

Jeanne placed the wool in Julie's basket. Placing her hand over Julie's on the handle, she said, "Please forgive me if I offended you. I don't think you're at all cowardly, just sensible. And, Joel, watch out for Big Auguste, the blacksmith. He has been looking for you. He's not a bad fellow, really. He just has to prove something by fighting everybody who comes as a stranger."

Julie frowned as she stepped into the street. She wished, unreasonably, that Jeanne were less pleasant and kind. As she picked out some onions in the market for Lucienne, she saw Auguste come out of the smithy door wearing a leather apron over his stocky chest. He greeted a man leading a limping horse. She kept moving behind the stalls and people, for she certainly wanted to avoid a showdown with Auguste.

As Julie turned toward home, a dog raced around the corner of a nearby house, barking at a cat that leaped up onto a windowsill and disappeared into the house. At that moment, she recognized Comrade, Philippe's dog. She tried to slip away, unseen by the dog who had once been her playmate, but the old dog was too near. With a frenzy of barking, the big dog lunged for her.

She decided to pretend fright and tried to ward off the eager animal. A glance backward revealed that Auguste and several others had turned to watch the disturbance. She grabbed her basket and ran for home, the barking Comrade still pursuing her. Laughter followed her from the square. She was glad the streets swallowed her quickly because Comrade caught her almost immediately. His overwhelming happiness to see her would have raised questions.

"Comrade, you old rascal! You must control yourself." she whispered to the exuberant dog. "Don't you see I'm a stranger, a young man you've never seen before?" The wagging tail and licking tongue denied this.

Counting the years, Julie decided Comrade must be at least ten years old. She remembered the romps they had enjoyed together with Philippe.

She jerked her arms from Comrade as she realized someone was watching from the shadows. She jumped up and tried to go on her way, but a cloaked man blocked her path. Looking up into a pair of twinkling black eyes, she gasped as she recognized Dr. Boulard. The unmistakable recognition in his eyes alarmed her.

Before he could speak, Julie stammered, "My name is Joel! I just came ... I'm new ... I work for Monsieur Jacques. I mean ...!" She felt panic. "I'm in a hurry, Doctor. Please let me pass."

He chuckled. "And how do you know I'm a doctor?"

"Your ... cloak?" she faltered.

"Now, now." He smiled at her confusion. "Tell me, do you always have that effect on strange dogs?"

"Yes, sir, I mean ... no, sir."

"It's no use, Julie," his voice was so low, she hardly heard. "You can trust me. How could you think you would fool your old doctor? Welcome home."

"Oh, Doctor Boulard!" How good it was to be called Julie.

"Your father needs you, my dear. I was afraid you wouldn't get here before ..."

As she strained to hear the doctor's words, they were interrupted. "Joel!" It was Lafayere.

Julie turned. "I've been looking for you. Come on." He gave a curious glance at the doctor, who excused himself and walked away.

"What were you talking about?" demanded Lafayere.

"He ... he was asking about Jacques. Said he was his doctor and hopes I'll help keep an eye on his health."

"Oh," the answer satisfied Lafayere. "But be careful, that man is under suspicion, too. It's a pity he's the only doctor in the village." Julie was glad the dog had darted back toward the square.

"Listen, I've got to have some information on Jacques right away. By tomorrow, in fact. You've got to pin that old man down today. Make him talk to you."

"You think he'll trust me so soon?"

"He's got to. I must have some information for the intendant. Some important people are coming to Aubusson tomorrow. You'd better uncover something by then!"

Chapter X
Forbidden Luxury

It rained that afternoon, and Julie was glad. The shadowy tapestry room was quiet and cozy with the rain beating on the windows and pouring off the roof. While she worked with her father, they talked of many things. He told her some harmless information that she could tell Lafayere. She didn't mention the tragic village scene she had witnessed that morning.

Lafayere was waiting for her when she came out that evening. There was enough truth in what Jacques had told her to satisfy the soldier. The names and facts that she repeated to him pleased him.

Lucas was grumbling at Lucienne when Julie and Lafayere entered the kitchen. "That huge pot of water is steaming up the kitchen," he complained. Lucienne explained, curtly, that since this was a tapisserie, she needed to heat her wool-dying water there. After supper, Julie helped Lucienne carry the water upstairs. The servant woman had more comfortable quarters than her master. This had once been Julie's room.

"'Tis a pity you've come home to a house where you can't even sleep in a good bed," moaned Lucienne, her eyes on Julie's face. Julie strolled solemnly around the room, remembering, rediscovering.

"No, Lucie, I'd rather be near Father. I've been away from him for so long. I want to spend every moment I can near him," she said gently. She started out the door.

"Mademoiselle, please. You must come to my room as soon as you can get free of those men," Lucienne insisted. "Come when nobody sees you, but come."

"More mysteries around here," Julie muttered as she hurried back down the stairs to the kitchen, where chores awaited her.

The men still sat around the table. She was amazed to see that Philippe had come in. She hadn't seen him since their arrival in Aubusson. Lafayere had placed his boots by the fireplace for her to polish. As she picked up a boot and applied goose grease to it, she was glad of the job. It gave her an excuse to hear what was going on.

As the conversation dealt with soldier talk, Julie wondered if Jacques' candle-extinguishing visitor would try to come tonight. She had examined the intriguing candle and found that it had a loose wick. By pulling this extra long wick into the candle from beneath it (or from outside the window, in this case), the flame could be extinguished. But that was the only mystery she had solved.

She thought she heard sounds outside. No one else seemed to notice. Lucas and Gautier fidgeted. Lafayere didn't even try to disguise his boredom when Philippe and Jacques guided the conversation into an argument about the cause and philosophy of war. Finally, Lafayere interrupted a long discourse by Philippe.

"Sir, I just remembered an errand I must do in the village. Do you mind if we leave you for a while?"

"An errand at the tavern," Julie thought. Lafayere failed to realize that Philippe and Jacques wanted to drive the dragoons away from their conversation and company.

"We'll not be long," promised the corporal, saluting from the doorway. "Thank you very much, sir."

When Lafayere and his two companions were out of hearing, Julie laughed softly. "Thank you, sir," she mimicked his voice. "I imagine Philippe feels more like saying that to them for leaving us. Those stupid fools!"

Philippe frowned and turned to Jacques. "Is it customary for one's apprentice to sit in with the master's visitors?" he said.

Jacques hesitated. "Our guest is right, Julie. You need your sleep, anyway. I'll see you in the morning."

Julie was furious with this man who could insult her so easily. Her every effort to be friendly with him was dashed aside. But Jacques' words were firm, and she chose to not argue. She didn't care to spend the evening with that unpleasant captain anyway.

Instead of going to bed across the hall, she tiptoed up the stairs to Lucienne's room. After rapping softly at her door, she slipped inside. The shutters were closed and the large pot of water was sitting in front of the fireplace where Lucie had built a tiny fire. When Julie saw fresh soap and clean drying cloths in Lucie's hands, she understood. Lucie's smiling eyes twinkled.

"Oh, Lucie," and she flung her arms around her servant's neck, "an honest-to-goodness bath. It's been ages since I had such a luxury."

"There now, you must be quiet, Ma Petite." Lucienne talked to her as though she were still eight years old, and she prepared her bath in the same manner. Completely happy, Julie surrendered herself to the brisk scrubbing and the wonderful hot water that Lucie poured over her.

"Do you know, Lucie, that not all of the fine court ladies believe in baths? It's quite out of fashion among some of them. But I shall never stop loving good clean scrubbings like those you gave me as a child. Lucie, you don't know how I've yearned for a good bath since putting on those ugly boy clothes."

Lucienne moved swiftly about, clucking her pleasure at waiting on her mademoiselle once more. When Julie was clean, she stood by the fire wrapped in fresh drying cloths and glanced disdainfully at the garments she had discarded, wishing she didn't have to put them on her clean body. She stretched out a hand toward them, reluctantly.

"No, no, Ma Petite, I have another surprise for you." Lucienne dug deeply into a basket of weaving wool, pulled out another set of peasant clothes, top and pants, and offered them to Julie. "Haven't you noticed how busily I've been sewing since you arrived?"

"You're so good, Lucie." She hesitated. "I suppose I should sleep in them, but ..."

Lucienne stepped over to a cupboard and pulled out a simple, sturdy nightgown. Julie was beside her almost immediately, staring over her shoulder into the cupboard.

"What's this," she asked, breathlessly, as she fingered the green cloth folded on the shelf. Impulsively, she pulled out a green brocade manteau, spilling a mass of lace and linen onto the floor.

Lucienne flushed. "No one knows those are there, Ma'am'selle. I saved them from the things your mother left. Your father would be angry if he knew."

"Lucie, look! A beautiful flounced skirt – and look at the lace on this manteau!" Only a few days ago Julie's wardrobe had included many elegant dresses. Yet, here she was, going wild over these precious, old-fashioned things.

"No, no, you mustn't," exclaimed Lucienne. Julie was putting on the dress. There was no stopping her. She stuffed the new boy clothes into the cupboard, as she pulled out the frills.

"She must have been my size," whispered Julie, as she stood in the center of the room, awed by the lovely costume. Then her mood changed, as though transformed by the fancy clothes.

"La, la, la, la," she trilled, twirling around the room, her manteau trailing behind her in a graceful train, the skirt bouncing and flowing. "Oh, Lucie, how do you like the lady?"

Lucienne stood to one side, tears streaming down her scarlet cheeks. She shook her head, fearfully. Her happiness at seeing Julie as a beautiful young woman overwhelmed her fear of discovery.

Julie ran her fingers through her damp hair, wondering how her short ringlets must look in place of the heavy powdered wig her mother wore.

"Am I boy or girl now, Madame," she inquired mischievously, planting a quick kiss on the wet cheeks of the servant.

"Oh, you're a girl, every bit of you," smiled Lucienne, dabbing at her eyes.

Suddenly a loud banging on the bedroom door caused Julie's gaiety to disappear. She and Lucienne exchanged terrified looks.

"Open this door! What's going on?" It was the voice of Lucas. The banging threatened to break down the door.

Lucienne sped to the fireside, brushed the clues of a bath out of sight, and dumped a concentrated red liquid into the bath water. Then she plopped Julie's old, discarded boy clothes into the kettle and put wool yarn on top of them. Julie leaped into the bed and pulled the covers up to her chin. Lucie stared at her red hands. She hurried to the bedside and flicked her hand at Julie sprinkling drops of red dye onto Julie's face.

"Now act sick," she hissed.

Julie closed her eyes when Lucienne opened the door. Through slitted lids, she saw an angry Lucas.

"Why didn't you open the door? Why was it bolted in the first place?" Then he saw the apprentice in Lucienne's bed. "What's he doing in here," he roared.

Lafayere and Gautier appeared in the doorway behind Lucas. Lucas strode toward the bed, but Lucienne intercepted him. "He's terribly sick," she insisted. "I just thought poor old blind Monsieur ought not to be exposed to this sick boy."

"How could he be sick? He was fine at supper." Lucas pushed her to one side.

Philippe strode into the room and said, "Who's sick?"

Lucas explained about hearing strange sounds and finding the locked door and the boy in Lucienne's bed. "This woman coddles him all the time in spite of our orders."

Philippe looked around the room as he answered, "If the boy's sick, maybe she's being helpful. Especially if she can get him well by morning."

"Naw, I'm not fooled. He's putting on because he sure wasn't sick at the supper table," Lucas grumbled.

Philippe stopped beside the bed. His strong hand felt Julie's forehead. She thought his eyes twinkled, and he almost smiled.

"Feel his head. Rather warm, wouldn't you say?"

Lucas put his hand, cold from the outdoors, on Julie's head, which was warm from her recent bath and exercise. At the same moment, he yelped, "Spots! He's got spots on his face!"

Gautier, who had never entered the room, dashed down the stairs, exclaiming, "Pox – he's got spots pox," his tongue too twisted to find the right word.

Lafayere looked worried. After all, small pox was one of the most dreaded curses of the day. Julie had once been told by one of Albert's soldier friends that soldiers feared being disfigured by the miserable pox more than dying in glorious battle.

Lucas left the bedside quickly. Lafayere said, "We'd better send for the doctor and see if it's the pox. He'll have to be moved from this house immediately if it is."

Philippe nodded, stroking his chin thoughtfully. "I'd hate to see you men exposed to the pox. Since the infection is already in the house, if it is pox, don't you think it would be better for you to move to the tavern until it's certain?"

Lafayere nodded eagerly. "We can come back tomorrow if it's safe. Are you sure it will be all right with the intendant?"

As Philippe started to follow Lafayere and Lucas out the door, he paused and looked back. Julie was almost sure he winked at her. I'm imagining things, she decided, as his broad back disappeared.

Her hand crept to her throat. Her fingers clutched at the cover and explored the stiff ruffles that must have been peeking out. Her eyes met Lucienne's.

"The lace was showing! Do you suppose Philippe knows what I was up to?" she asked Lucienne.

The woman smiled. "Probably, but he's the only one who had sense enough to see through our trick." Julie and Lucienne laughed delightedly at their joke on the hated dragoons.

Chapter XI
The Plot Revealed

The firelight danced on the walls of the room and reflected off the window panes, creating dozens of tiny bonfires. The chill of the October evenings and early mornings required a fire.

Julie stretched her arms lazily above her head. "Is it safe to get up now?"

Lucienne's face crinkled with smiles as she nodded her assent. Julie changed from her elaborate costume into the simple nightgown, this time without argument. "Why do I have to sleep in here tonight, instead of downstairs with my father?"

"Those are my orders."

"Has Father gone, too?"

"No, he never leaves here, but I guess he's too busy for you tonight."

"Has Philippe gone?"

"I guess so." Then Lucie began to chuckle. "Those dragoons really did leave in a hurry."

Julie was quiet for a few moments. "Is someone with Father?" she finally asked.

"I haven't seen anyone, have you?"

"Well, then, I'll put on a wrapper and go sit with him. We have so little time together when the dragoons are here."

"No, no, you must stay here," urged Lucienne, her voice suddenly commanding. "I mean, please stay here, M'am'selle. Your father will come when he's ready to see you."

"Lucie, what's going on? When am I to be let in on some of these secrets?" Julie asked. Lucienne shook her head and was silent.

"Please, then, let's talk about my father. I saw Dr. Boulard today, and he hinted that your master has been gravely ill. What did he mean, Lucie?"

Lucienne looked sorrowfully at Julie. "I'm sorry, Ma Petite. I can't talk about his health either. His orders."

Julie puckered her brows and rubbed the nape of her neck. Before she could analyze the uncomfortable worry deep inside, she heard footsteps ascending the stairway. She started to dive back into bed.

"It's alright. Your father is coming," Lucienne said.

Jacques hesitated at the door, stopping to locate Julie. She glided to his side, and he put his arms around her.

"Oh, Julie, this couldn't have worked better had you planned it. Only, it was a foolish risk you took. Doc is coming," he added.

"But I'm not sick!"

"There are those who must continue to think you are," Jacques reminded her. The doctor entered the room, and they all laughed again at the joke on the dragoons.

"We'll stall the dragoons for a day or two. I'll tell them I have to be sure. This will give Julie time to get some rest and build up her strength for what's ahead. She looks run down from her travels," Doctor Boulard said.

Julie lowered herself to a stool by the fire. Jacques sat on a chair near her, and the doctor leaned against the mantle. Lucienne left the room with the wet wool and the discarded clothing.

"Two days is all we need," said Jacques.

Julie sat up, alert. "That's the day you send your tapestries to the king's agents at the Lyons Fair," she said.

The two men fell silent. "She doesn't know?" the doctor finally demanded.

"I haven't had an opportunity to tell her the plan," answered Jacques. "After all, she was only added to the plan tonight."

"To what?" asked Julie.

Jacques leaned over, found Julie's hand, and caressed it as he talked. "The trip to Lyons is only a bluff. As you know, Jeanne Lafaud, her fourteen-year-old brother, and Auguste Craone are to accompany the tapestries, along with a military escort. You've been given permission to go, too. Due to your performance as a spy for Lafayere, no doubt." He smiled wryly.

"I don't want to go to Lyons and leave you," she insisted.

"Listen to me. Lyons isn't the destination, La Rochelle is." Julie's hand trembled. Her father grasped it tighter and hurried on. "Another thing not known to the authorities, instead of four youths there will be fifteen, mostly children!"

"That's impossible!" Julie exclaimed.

"Don't interrupt, Julie." His voice resonated with urgency. "These are the last children from the Huguenot families who want to leave France for a land of religious freedom. Many are going to Holland and America. The Huguenot people of Aubusson have planned and saved for this tremendous gamble for many months. The parents have counted the risk and the heartache of separation. It's impossible for everyone to leave, so we decided our youth must have the opportunity for a new life in a new world. You are to be a part of this group."

Julie stared from one face to the other, stunned.

Doctor Boulard spoke. "Only you young folks can succeed in this escape. We older folks are watched and restricted. Besides, we have few years left and you have many. Imagine the bright future that lies ahead for you. Think of it – freedom!"

"We prepared our children for a new life without letting them know. Auguste can earn his living as a blacksmith, Jeanne and her brothers as weavers. Even you, Julie, have enough training to become a governess to some family in the New World."

"Wait," cried Julie. "You can't mean … Father, you're not going?"

"Of course not, Julie."

"Then I'll not even consider it. Why, we just found each other. How could you expect me to desert you? Don't you believe I love you, even yet?"

Jacques smiled. "Julie, I never doubted your love: love requires no proof. I never dreamed I'd ever ask you to sacrifice so much, but I beg you to take your place in this escape."

"My place is here with you, Father. Don't, please don't ask me to leave you. I have lived for this return to Aubusson. I'll never, never leave again!"

Jacques shook his head. "Julie, you don't know the dangerous, impossible life we lead. Especially the women. You must go!"

The doctor interrupted. "Julie, it's impossible for any of us to go with you, most impossible for your father. Can't you see that?"

"His blindness is no more a handicap than being a child," she insisted.

"But Jacques has more to cope with than his blindness. He hasn't let me tell you, but I believe it's time."

Jacques groped for Doctor Boulard. "No, it isn't necessary! She'll go without that."

Julie grew more apprehensive with each moment. "What are you trying to tell me?" She moistened her dry lips.

"Your father has an incurable disease. He doesn't have more than a few weeks at most. Now do you see why you must do this thing for him? He wants to live on in you —in a free land."

Julie slid onto the floor in front of her father, and grasped his knees. His regular coughing, his feverish skin, his thin body, all of which she had noted since her return, supported the doctor's statement. Jacques caressed her tousled head as she sobbed, "Then he needs me more than ever. You cannot make me leave Aubusson. I shall not! Father needs me."

"Julie, Julie. It's enough that God spared me long enough to have you with me once more, to know what a fine, brave young woman you've become. The bravest choice you must make is to leave Aubusson. The other families have had to make the same choice. Are we weaker than they?"

"But, Father, they've always had one another. They've probably grown even closer, sharing this dream. You and I have been cruelly separated, and I can't bear to leave you now!"

Jacques bent his head over Julie's. She felt his body shake with emotion. "You must! You must! You cannot stay," he murmured.

The doctor straightened himself and spoke sharply. "Julie, as Jacques' doctor, I must forbid you to defy his wishes. The hope that you would escape is the only thing that has kept him alive. He has been the inspiration in the entire planning. You're taking his fondest dream from him!"

Julie looked up through tear-filled eyes. "Then if he's so important, he deserves to go and be our leader!"

Doctor Boulard stamped his foot. "That is impossible as we told you. Why must you be so stubborn?"

"It's all right, Frederick," Jacques said. "I'll handle her. You get back to your family. And thank you for coming over and for helping us postpone the return of our unwelcome guests."

After the doctor left, Julie remained on the floor cuddled against Jacques while he told her more of the plans. She listened quietly to please him, but she resolved that she wouldn't desert her father a second time.

"We saved a place for you, as my daughter. I've had a hard time, I tell you, winning permission from my Huguenot friends to include my apprentice in my Julie's place. The young children who aren't commissioned to go to the fair will be spirited out to a prearranged place outside the village during the night, two nights hence. Early the next morning you four young folks will leave your soldier escort. Incidentally, the outlaws will also hear rumors that will plant them in the same vicinity. We hope the soldiers and the outlaws will keep each other busy while you and the children move away in the opposite direction."

"Who's going?"

"Besides Jeanne, Didier, and Auguste, there are the other three Lafaud brothers, the postman's two daughters, Doctor Boulard's three sons, the two daughters of Joseph, the lawyer—and you."

Julie had counted them off, trying to remember their approximate ages. "That's only fourteen."

"Are you sure?" Jacques smiled, unconcerned.

"Aren't they young to make such a dangerous trip?"

"No greater than their danger here. They are our most promising young people. Aubusson will live on in them, wherever they go. We're staking all our dreams in them."

"And their parents?" The boldness and the unselfishness of this grand scheme awed Julie, though she did not intend to take part in it.

"Their parents feel honored that their children are worthy of being included. If possible, the parents will leave France later, but it's unlikely. You see, we have very reliable information that the king will soon revoke the Edict of Nantes, the agreement that is supposed to grant us freedom of worship in our own cities and villages. Our king hasn't kept the rules of the agreement, and that has made life difficult. Now he's taking away our last hope, by revoking this law. He will forbid all departures from the country. We hope our children will reach safety before this revocation takes place."

"Are you sure the king would do that?" Julie had been taught in Valjean to revere and agree always with King Louis Fourteenth.

"Another reason for the urgency, Julie, is the danger to our children right here. According to the law, the State can take children who are over seven years old from their Huguenot parents and put them into a convent or monastery. Parents have no legal right to see or communicate with their stolen children, who usually disappear from their lives. Soldiers dragged away Doctor Boulard's only daughter a year ago. She was just ten years old. We live in fear that authorities will seize his sons any day. Our children must escape to safety!"

Julie stared through misty eyes into the fire. A few days ago, she would have protested that such things couldn't be true in France. Since her departure from Valjean, she had seen and learned much. What a cruel world she had chosen by leaving the sheltered life of the chateau. If only Jacques could leave with her, she would welcome the challenge of starting life in a new land with new ideals.

"Father, is there no way to include you in the escape?" she pleaded.

"No, Julie. Not only because of my physical weakness, but for other reasons as well. With only fifteen places on the escape ship we must save all of them for young people."

"But how can this plan succeed without you to lead?"

"The leader you have is worth fifty of me!" Jacques was chuckling. Julie looked up, horrified that he could laugh at such a moment.

"That's impossible. Who is he?"

Jacques couldn't answer at first. A severe coughing spell seized him and for some while he couldn't speak. He was even more hoarse and short of breath when he resumed, "That you cannot know. In fact, very few of those in on the plan know all the details. You must not mention anything about this to anyone in the village."

Jacques kissed the top of Julie's head and left the room just as Lucienne returned. Julie climbed into her childhood bed and snuggled under the covers. "Lucie, what about you? What will become of you when everything happens?"

"Don't worry about me, Ma Petite. An unimportant old woman like me can disappear the fastest of all. I'll go to my relatives 'way up in the Auvergne mountains when I'm no longer needed here."

Julie shuddered a little; dread settled upon her. Lucie hadn't mentioned Jacques. Did she think he would lead the escape or did she, too, believe that he had only weeks, or days left to live?

Chapter XII
The Monastery

When Julie awoke next morning, the sun was shining brightly upon a patch of scrubbed floor near the window. After stretching lazily, she started to roll out of bed, then remembered, "Oh, I'm still sick."

She wondered if the soldiers had returned and if they believed she had smallpox. She felt tense and excited as she remembered that in less than forty-eight hours the Aubusson Plan of Escape would unfold.

Rolling over onto her stomach, Julie grabbed a shoe and rapped briskly on the floor to let the household know she was awake. The soft, padded steps of Lucienne ascended the stairway.

"Are you awake, Ma Petite?" Lucienne asked needlessly as she came through the door.

"How long must I stay up here, Lucie?"

"Good news," the servant answered. "The dragoons left Aubusson and won't be back before tomorrow. They went to escort somebody important. No one knows who it can be."

"Good. Now we'll see if my new clothes fit so I can join Father." She washed her face in the basin of water and ran a brush through her hair. How much easier it was to care for this natural hairstyle. She remembered the long tedious hours she and Ularie had spent dressing her hair at Valjean and in Paris.

Lucienne watched anxiously as Julie put on the new smock and trousers. She beamed with pride as Julie winked and raced down the stairway. Julie threw open the door to Jacques' workroom.

"Father! Father!" She stopped in surprise as her father sprang to his feet, startled.

He spoke to her sharply, "Stop!"

Julie stood very still.

"You must never enter my room without announcing yourself," Jacques resumed his usual gentle tone. "I'm sorry, Julie, I didn't mean to sound angry."

She started toward him again. He sensed her movements, for he said, "Come no farther, Julie. I'm coming to you."

Julie waited, wondering why Jacques should object to her joining him. Jacques covered up the loom on which he had been working. This loom, always covered with a gray cloth, stood in a dark corner of the large room. Usually piles of wool lay on top of the cloth. Julie had never given the loom a second thought until her father mysteriously kept her away from it. Was this where her father worked late each night and early each morning? Was it also kept hidden from the eyes of the dragoons? What was so special about that tapestry?

In response to her curiosity, Jacques explained, "This is another work which I must complete before the cart leaves for the fair. I don't want you to see it yet."

"Father, whom do you suppose the dragoons have gone to meet?" Julie feared that there was a sinister connection between the arrival of the visitors, the hints that her father was in danger—and the plan.

Jacques uncovered the almost completed tapestry he always worked when she was with him. "It doesn't really matter what dignitaries come to Aubusson now because our plans are nearly final. It's a great blessing to have the dragoons gone and the intendant preoccupied for the last few hours. We will know who the visitors are tomorrow."

"You don't think it will mean more danger – to you or to the plan?"

"The danger is already so great, does it really matter? Since the soldiers are gone, we can admit the pox diagnosis was a mistake. You can go into the village. You must keep your ears open for any word of what is afoot. Also, I need you to deliver a message to Monsieur Lafaud for me."

Julie stopped by the kitchen to eat the fragrant pork and flat hearth cakes Lucienne was preparing for her. "Has Father eaten?" she asked.

"He ate his usual mite." Lucienne screwed up her mouth with disapproval. "I gave up on him long time ago."

Julie took her first bite and looked up to compliment Lucienne. "What's the matter?" she asked. The woman's arms were crossed against her breast, and her frowning countenance made plain her displeasure.

"Didn't you forget something?" she asked, shaking a finger in Julie's face.

Julie was genuinely puzzled. "Oh, thank you, Lucie, for the tasty breakfast," she floundered, confused.

"Not me, Mademoiselle, don't thank me. Thank Him."

Julie stared back at Lucienne, trying to comprehend this strange behavior. She was causing Lucienne pain, and she had no idea why.

"Ma Petite, you mean you aren't one of us?" Lucienne's wrinkled cheeks provided furrows for the tears that trickled from her reproachful eyes. Julie, understanding at last, felt embarrassed and more confused than ever.

"I'm sorry, Lucie, I guess I've forgotten a lot of things since I went away. You say what I'm supposed to," she mumbled.

Lucienne was adamant. She shook her head and dabbed the tears away. "If you knew what a miracle every meal in this house was, you wouldn't need a body to do your thanking for you. Now, you bow that head and you talk to Him, just like you was thanking me a minute ago."

Julie bent her head meekly. After an embarrassing moment, she stammered, "Thank you very much for this food," and then to her own surprise, she added, "… and thank you, too, for bringing me home and to Jacques and Lucie …"

"Amen," whispered Lucie, and her old face was beaming again when Julie looked up. She finished her breakfast and hurried back to Jacques for directions. When she tried the door this time, it was bolted.

Jacques opened the door, but before she could enter, he came into the hall. He shut the door carefully behind him.

"I'm ready for you to go to the wool shop. Tell Monsieur Lafaud that the fowls roost here five hours late tonight. Can you remember that?"

Julie nodded, then remembered her father couldn't see her. "Yes, Father. The fowls roost here at five hours tonight." More mystery, she thought.

"No, you didn't repeat the message correctly. Listen, and don't leave out a word. The fowls roost here five hours late tonight."

Julie repeated it correctly three times. Jacques walked with her to the outside entrance where she stooped to put on her shoes.

"Julie, be careful in the village. Even my own people mistrust you. Deliver my message and then come on home. You need not try to discover the identity of the guest that the intendant is expecting."

Julie patted his arm and planted a kiss on each scarred cheek. Then she hurried to the Lafaud Wool Shop.

"Are ye certain, Lad? Are those his very words? It wouldn't go well with ye if ye be wrong." Julie hid her peeved resentment from the suspicious Lafaud. No one trusted her.

"Those are his very words, I'm certain. He instructed me very carefully," she said. Finally, he was satisfied.

She could see through the curtained doorway into the family living quarters. Madame Lafaud appeared briefly in the doorway. Seeing her husband with a visitor, she withdrew quickly, but not before Julie noticed her stricken, yet composed face. Madame knows she must lose all her children, Julie thought.

Two small boys, nine and eight years old, rushed through the front door. "Papa! Papa!" shouted the older one. "Monsieur Krause gave George a sweet, and he didn't share with me!"

"But Pierre wasn't there, Papa, or he would have gotten a sweetie, too," the little boy argued.

Monsieur Lafaud ushered his sons through the doorway so their mother could settle their problem. "Do they know what is in store for them," wondered Julie. "Have the little ones been told?"

Still wondering, Julie turned to leave the shop. Suddenly a youth about her size confronted her. He stared intently at her with unfriendly eyes. She guessed he must be Didier, the oldest Lafaud son.

Christian, about twelve years old, entered the shop behind him. Though Julie nodded and spoke, they didn't return her greeting. She felt Didier's eyes on her as she walked from the shop. The boy need not be so concerned, she thought. She had no intention of joining the escapees. Still, it annoyed her to be accepted only through Jacques' considerable influence.

Julie stopped beside an old fountain in the square. When coaxed, the fountain spewed forth streams of water from the two lions' heads mounted in the center. A foot-deep trough from which the horses could drink encircled the fountain. She rinsed her hands in the sparkling water and drank a cool draught of running water from her palms.

She debated Jacques' advice to return home immediately. She was strongly tempted to prove herself to Jacques' cause. The intendant had an important secret, a secret that could mean alarming danger to

Jacques and his friends.

Philippe's dog trotted into the square. He headed directly to the fountain, hardly glancing at Julie. When he had slurped his fill, he greeted her calmly. She fondled his ears and whispered, "Where's your master, old boy, your glorious, puffed up Monsieur?"

As if in answer, Philippe rode into the square, dismounted, and entered the Lafaud shop. Julie decided suddenly that it was her duty to linger awhile in the square and watch the intendant's house. She denied even to herself that Lafaud's shop was the real attraction.

She sat down beneath a young oak tree, and Comrade settled beside her. Some villagers looked at her curiously as they passed by, others ignored her. She recognized no one from her past.

Twin boys crossed the square, engrossed in a collection of stones one of them carried. They stopped beside Comrade. One twin dropped on one knee to pat the dog; the other stood examining the strange boy whom Comrade had befriended.

"Aren't you the boy who lives with Monsieur Jacques?" asked the one standing, his bright blue eyes squinting above chubby, extremely red cheeks. The other pair of identical blue eyes joined in the scrutiny.

"That's right, I'm Joel. What are you called?"

"Thomas and Zachary Boulard," the dog-patter lisped. "I'm Thomas. You can tell by my lost tooths." He drew back his lips to reveal a gaping hole where three teeth should have been.

"Oh, you're the doctor's sons," said Julie, looking at them with real interest. She judged they must be about nine years of age.

A loud commotion arose in front of the inn, which adjoined the intendant's house. "Get out and go on," the proprietor yelled at a fat, dusty peddler. I don't have any room for you, and if you don't stop trying to make trouble, I'll call the dragoons."

The man whined, "Full up, ye say. Ye believe not that I've the price of a room. Ye think yon place is too fine for a merchant like me."

The innkeeper disappeared inside and left the man muttering to himself. The peddler adjusted the pack on his back and shuffled toward the fountain. "He hopes a rich traveler will come along and pay more than I will," he complained.

Thomas spoke up. "No, Old Mac really does have a full inn. This morning I heard him and the intendant arguing. Old Mac wanted all the dragoons to move out to make room for some people who are coming to town."

The peddler lost interest and shuffled away. But Julie turned eagerly to the child. "What did the intendant say, Thomas?"

"He said the dragoons would stay in the inn. He said he has made other arrangements for the great ones."

"The soldiers don't have to pay the innkeeper," explained Julie, but her mind leaped ahead, wondering where the guests would stay if they did not stay at the only inn in town.

"Did you hear the names of the guests?" she asked Thomas.

Thomas shook his head. "No. Papa asked me that, too, and when I came back to find out, Old Mac chased me away."

Julie thought, "There are no fine homes in Aubusson because the de Vauve home is closed. Philippe is staying at his hunting cottage. The intendant sleeps at the inn. The chateau is in ruins, except for the monastery the monks have built there ..." Julie stopped. "That's it – it has to be," she said aloud as she jumped up and left the two children.

She entered a narrow street that twisted up one of the steep hills. She walked past the Church of Notre Dame and finally reached the hill's summit. She paused near the walls of the chateau ruins.

Richilieu, the minister of government, destroyed the Chateau of Aubusson a generation ago. This shrewd minister, to crush the power of the country nobles, tore down all feudal castles so local rebels couldn't retreat into them to defy the king.

Some fifteen years ago, monks started a monastery within the ruins and rebuilt the walls. They used the old chateau materials to erect several buildings, including barns and living quarters. All women were banned from the property, of course. But occasionally the child Julie sneaked over the wall with Philippe to play in the huge trees and to hide, with terrified excitement, from the unsuspecting monks.

Julie remembered that the monastery had often entertained visiting men, especially high ranking church officials. The monks keep special apartments for them. The mysterious guests must be lodging here.

"If only I could enter," she moaned to herself. As she kicked, frustrated, at a stone, Julie realized that she could enter. Wasn't she, to all concerned, a male? Of course, if she was discovered – she shuddered to think of her fate. Breaking a sacred law of the monks like that! But this was more or less war. Julie felt she must take the risk to get inside and find out the identity of the important company.

A persistent yapping noise drew her attention. A few yards down the hill she saw a lively young dog leaping about, attacking an imaginary enemy. Julie ran down to the puppy, befriended him, and scooped him under her arm. Returning to the gate, she marched up and rang the bell. Several moments passed before a stooped old man responded.

"Hello, I found this runaway dog. I believe he belongs here. Are you missing a dog?" she asked the man who opened the gate.

"Alors, no! No dogs missing around here," and the old man gave a kick at one of the half dozen dogs that were barking at Julie from inside the gate. "In fact, Mignon just had puppies and I'm for getting rid of 'em. No, no, no! We don't want no more dogs!"

Julie stooped and released the squirming dog, which raced away. "Do you mean it?" she spoke eagerly. "Do you really have puppies to give away?"

The old man was in the act of closing the gate. He stopped when he heard her excited question. "Well, yes, but they're too little to give away yet."

"Oh, please, may I see them?"

The man hesitated. "Oh, I guess so." He led her toward the stables at the back of the property. "Don't see why the monks want so many dogs, anyway." Julie suspected the old man was much fonder of the dogs than he pretended.

Julie looked carefully around as they walked toward the barns. When they reached the litter of pups, Julie bent over them, exclaiming as a lad should over the irresistible baby creatures. "I like this one best," she said, burying her cheek in the coat of a turbulent little black ball.

"Well, come back in a couple weeks, and I'll give him to you. How 'bout spreading the word and helping me find homes for all of 'em?"

"I will," Julie promised. She made no move to leave but kept playing with the pups. The old man finally sat on a stump near the barn doorway and watched her.

"Things seem pretty quiet around here, for a bunch of pups, I mean," observed Julie. The old man said nothing. She tried again. "You don't suppose a boy like me could get a job here that would pay a few pennies?"

"Oh, so that's it," and the man's eyes twinkled. "Nope, don't need no help, m'self. ' Course, sometimes they need extra hands inside, but not often."

"Do you suppose they might hire me sometimes, just for a few hours at a time?"

"Fact is, if you come around on th' morrow morning they might be right glad to hire a boy, if he's a mind to work. But the work's temporary, you understand. Whose boy are you?"

"I'm a new apprentice in one of the tapisseries, but my master will be glad for me to make a little extra at other jobs," she replied. She stood up and gave one last hug to the little black pup. "I'll come by like you said, late tomorrow," she added, deliberately.

"You come by too late, you won't get no job," warned the old man. "Be here afore noon when everything's in commotion over the company."

"Company? Here? In a monastery?" Julie tried to sound scornful. The old man rose to the bait.

"And why not here? I'll have you know, Laddie, that we've slept the Bishop of Bourges, the Count of Berri – and tomorrow we're gonna top them all with the Marquis de Feuillarde and the Abbot of Clugny!" Suddenly remembering himself, he leaned over and cautioned, "But don't ye mention that to nobody, Laddie. If you want to work here, you have to keep your mouth shut about what goes on inside these walls."

Somehow, Julie forced her shaking knees to carry her out the gate. When the gate slammed shut, she ran down the hill. Her feet could not out-race her thumping heart: the marquis, here! Was he searching for her? Did he suspect she was hiding in her hometown? Or was he traveling here to vent his hate and frustration on her defenseless, blind father?

Julie determined to keep a wide distance between herself and the monastery. The old man would think nothing of it if she didn't show up tomorrow. At least she had the information she had sought.

She didn't slow down when she reached the square. She wasn't even aware when she shoved against pedestrians or startled them, she was so absorbed in rushing home to Jacques. As she hurried along, she jostled someone who was leaning against the wall. His arm shot out quickly and grabbed her smock. She recoiled in fear as she gazed up into the glaring eyes of Auguste Craone!

Chapter XIII
The Fight

Auguste smelled of smoke and hot metal, of horses and sweat. One vise-like hand hurt the back of Julie's neck. His narrow, suspicious eyes leered from his flushed face.

"Ah, ha! It's the little apprentice! The little apprentice who beat a whole battalion of highway robbers. The little apprentice who was just seen entering the monastery on top of the hill. Now why should he be in such a hurry, what?"

Julie's trembling beneath his strong grip no doubt encouraged him. He half dragged her to the clearing in the square. A group of people near the water fountain set down their water vessels to watch the commotion.

"Why don't you pick on somebody your own size?" Julie muttered.

"My own size? Ha, what matters a man's stature? Surely anybody who can stand off a whole band of robbers isn't afraid of one puny fellow like me?"

Julie flushed and the crowd laughed. Terror seized her as she realized a fight with this bully was inevitable. Surely the rough encounter would reveal her secret. Should she slink away? After all, everyone thought she was a coward. She decided this was the safest plan though hateful to her. She just hoped she could escape Auguste's determination to humble her.

A horse galloped into the square and stopped in front of them. Julie recognized Chestnut even before she looked up to see Philippe's stern face. Comrade was there, growling playfully, nuzzling first Julie, then Auguste.

"Unhand the lad, Craone," Philippe commanded.

"Why should I? He crashed into me on yonder rue and the bumpkin shall pay. Besides, he's stuck up and sneaky." Julie was surprised to see such spirit in Auguste when confronted by Philippe, his superior.

"The boy is a coward and not worth your trouble. If you injure him, he will be in no shape to work for Jacques."

"Everyone knows he's a coward, and they also suspect that his service to Jacques is all fake."

Philippe frowned. Julie tried to convince herself that he was insulting her only for her own safety. Or was it for his safety? How would he look if Joel the apprentice turned out to be the hunted daughter of Jacques, hated leader of Huguenots?

She looked at Philippe with a new insight. Phillipe had made her endure all the lies and insults to hide her identity, not for her own and Jacques' sake, but for his own safety. Phillipe had paid his debt to his old friend by delivering his daughter to Aubusson. Phillipe had no intention of becoming involved with the daughter or her dangerous father.

Auguste had loosened his grip on her during the argument between the two young men. Philippe suddenly urged his horse between Julie and Auguste, forcing them apart.

"Run for home, Joel! Run!" Philippe shouted.

But the move had surprised Julie as well as Auguste. She hesitated until it was too late. Auguste grabbed her again, tighter than ever. Deciding to trust luck and wits and even Lucienne's God, if He were interested, Julie declared boldly, "Let me go, you swine! I'll fight you!"

Philippe stared, unbelieving, at her, but he couldn't prevent the battle. Auguste released Julie. He backed up and rubbed his hands together. "Watch the little rooster get squashed, unless he turns tail and runs," he taunted.

In the few seconds that they faced each other, Julie didn't focus on Auguste alone. She sized up the location of the fountain and looked for Comrade. He was easy to find. He had sensed the excitement and was dashing around barking excitedly.

If only Comrade remembered! He was older, but he was her only hope right now. Years ago in a similar situation, she pulled a trick on Auguste in this very square with the help of the dog. Auguste constantly pestered Julie and the other little girls in the village until, with Philippe's help, she taught Comrade a trick. At a signal, Comrade learned to crouch behind Philippe, and then Julie would push Philippe over the dog's body so that he tripped and fell. She used this ruse on Auguste one day in the square, much to Auguste's chagrin.

Just in time, she saw Auguste lunge. Using her desperation and superior agility, she dodged nimbly and danced slowly toward the fountain. Auguste followed, watching for a chance to lunge again. He swaggered with confidence, certain of his advantage. She shouted insulting names, arousing Comrade with old familiar phrases. Auguste, grimly quiet, smiled smugly. Comrade responded to Julie's excited cries. He cocked his head, and he barked occasionally, watching her closely. She felt encouraged. She noted fleetingly that Philippe also watched, seated haughtily on his horse. She couldn't read his blank face but knew that he must feel frantic with worry.

Julie now stood against the fountain's edge. As Auguste taunted her for letting herself be trapped against a barrier, she chanted certain words to Comrade, who drew slowly nearer, lowering himself to his belly.

As Auguste lunged, she dodged again. He had expected this and avoided plunging into the fountain. But he misjudged her movements and she spun away from him. He turned and crouched because Julie, also in a crouch, was creeping toward him. He looked as if he expected to end the fight quickly.

"Comrade! Down him!" Julie cried.

In an instant, the dog sped the remaining inches to crouch close behind the surprised Auguste's legs. In the same instant, Julie charged Auguste and, though he tried to grapple with her, he received her headlong rush in his stomach and sprawled over the crouching dog into the village fountain.

The villagers roared with laughter. Everything had happened so quickly, they hadn't realized Comrade's part in the plot. But one person had.

As Julie ran her hand gratefully over Comrade's head, she glanced into the fountain pool where Auguste still sat, his wet face reflecting astonishment. As Julie met his eyes, a wave of apprehension swept over her. The risk saved her from exposure to the village, but she saw clearly from the shocked awakening in Auguste's eyes that here was one who suddenly knew her secret. He, as well as Comrade, remembered a trick played on a summer's day many years ago.

She whirled around and hurried toward home. Before she could get out of the square, Auguste scrambled out of the fountain. With a few quick strides, he caught up with her. He threw a dripping wet arm around her shoulders.

Julie heard laughter from the square. She gritted her teeth and hurried on. She felt Auguste's hands fingering the padding Lucienne had given her for her shoulders. She briefly noted Philippe's black look as she and Auguste left the square together and entered the little street leading toward the bridge.

Auguste didn't say a word but his arm dropped to his side. He kept pace with her until they crossed the bridge. Then he took her arm and guided her to a path at the river's edge, which also led to Jacques' home. When they were out of sight of everyone, he stepped in front of her. She was breathing hard from exertion, excitement, and dread. But his eyes were soft and friendly.

"Mademoiselle Julie! How was I to know? How you have fooled us all. Can you ever forgive me?"

Julie sat down weakly upon a fallen log, spent with relief. Was it possible that this young man apologizing, beseeching her with humility, was the same arrogant young contender she had faced in desperation only moments before?

"Then you won't tell on me, Auguste." She wanted reassurance.

"Mademoiselle, you know I won't tell on you. There's no one I care for more than your father. I'd give my life for him or for anyone belonging to him. But, oh, how blind I've been!"

"It's everyone's blindness that ensures my safety, Auguste. Don't be so embarrassed!"

"You don't understand, Mademoiselle," his rough voice broke. "I have fought every effort to include you in the escape plans. I knew there was something strange about you and I was convinced that you were a spy. When you were seen entering the old chateau-monastery, I was sure of it."

Julie decided impulsively that she could trust Auguste. She hadn't realized how alone she had felt with only Jacques and Lucienne to confide in, and neither of them was sympathetic with what she must do.

"I went to the chateau to learn what I could about tomorrow's visitors. They are to stay there."

"Of course, why didn't we think of that," Auguste said. "Do you know who's coming?"

Julie hesitated. She wasn't sure she should tell this to anyone but her father. Still, she wanted to trust this impetuous, strong young man who could be a sturdy ally.

Auguste looked at her intently. "Well?" he urged.

"Two important guests are coming: the Abbot of Clugny and the Marquis de Fuillarde." She watched Auguste to see if the latter name meant anything to him.

"That is the man who is offering a reward for your capture!" he exclaimed. "And he and the abbot are two of the fiercest enemies of the Huguenots. I don't like this at all! Why should they come at *this* time?"

Deep in thought as he gazed across the river, Auguste pursed his lips. "Mademoiselle Julie?"

"Yes?"

"Don't you think we should keep this from your father?"

Julie flinched. Had she confided in the wrong person? Was her trust misplaced? Jacques had said the town was full of spies, even among his own people.

"Why should we? He must know," she replied.

"It's true he's our leader, but I'm thinking of him more than our cause right now. Just think what effect this will have upon him since his daughter is now in more danger than ever."

She wanted to believe in Auguste's sincerity. She saw his logic. She, too, wished to shield Jacques from unnecessary suffering.

Auguste continued, "On the other hand, he's the wisest and greatest mind among us. He has always taught us to put the Faith above all personal matters. The danger will increase for all of us, even for Jacques. Use your own judgment, Mademoiselle," he sighed.

Julie relaxed. Gratified to see such devotion toward her father, she decided to share her own burdensome problem with Auguste.

"Auguste, tell me, is there another one in Aubusson who might be included in the escape plan, another child, I mean?"

"Oh, no! This has been planned for months, and fifteen is the limit."

"No, I mean are there substitutes standing by to fill in just in case someone can't make it?"

"But everyone must make it. We base all our plans on faith. You were allotted a spot only because, for Jacques' sake, we had reserved a place for his daughter." He bowed his head again. "And I fought so hard against the idea of Joel the apprentice going. I gave in only because Jacques insisted."

"But there has to be someone else. Surely you've made allowances for last minute substitutions!"

Auguste looked up at Julie. "What's bothering you, Mademoiselle? Do you know something I should know?"

"It's just that I can't go. I've decided to stay here with my father. I have found him again, and he needs me so much. Things will go hard for him when all of you leave. I feel my duty is to stay!"

He was quiet. He looked down at the ground. When he lifted his dark eyes to hers, they were tender and sad.

"You've been away and don't know our ways. You have no right to make that decision. The group has decided and especially, Jacques, our leader. You have to go with us."

"No!" she insisted, disappointed that Auguste, whom she had thought so independent, would not see it her way. She remained determined to enlist his aid.

Auguste suddenly lifted his head and stared downstream at the bridge. Julie followed his gaze and saw Philippe watching them from Chestnut's back.

"He knows you, of course," whispered Auguste, though no one could possibly have heard him. Julie nodded.

"Uh, huh – I just can't figure him out. He's so different since he's come home. I wouldn't trust him, Mademoiselle. He shouldn't have allowed me to get you into a fight."

"But he's wounded and couldn't physically prevent you," said Julie, surprised to find herself defending Philippe, whom she

~ Page 127 ~

suspected, too.

Auguste looked at her, then avoided her eyes. "That wouldn't have stopped me," he said softly.

Julie agreed silently. "But he did try to keep you from fighting me when he brought his horse between us."

"I think he's been hateful toward you," Auguste snorted, and Julie was glad to have someone on her side.

"Well, maybe he's had other reasons," she smiled.

"I don't think you should trust him," Auguste repeated, and then he slipped into the nearby bushes and disappeared.

Julie continued her return home. She still hadn't decided what to do about her news. Could her father stand such a blow?

Chapter XIV
Tragedy

Julie didn't mention her encounter with Auguste that night at dinner. It was a happy meal, in spite of the clouds of danger that she saw hovering over their cottage. They feasted on a tasty omelet, enjoying the absence of the coarse dragoons. When they had eaten their fill, Jacques folded his hands on the table and said, "Tell me about your day, Julie. Did you get any information?"

She hesitated. Should she report her bad news so he could prepare for trouble? "Yes, Father, I visited the monastery." Jacques reacted in surprise, and she continued quickly, "I guessed that the guests might stay there, and I was right."

"Did you find out who is coming?"

"Yes. The Marquis de Feuillarde and the Abbot de Clugny."

Jacques gripped the edge of the table, and his face whitened, making the scars more terrible than ever. "Are you certain?"

"That appears to be the truth, Father, but don't worry. He won't find me!"

"If only you left tomorrow. We must keep you out of sight, Julie. Under no circumstances must we let our plan fail for you now!" She was almost sorry she had told her father. She watched him, distressed by his pathetic helplessness, yet awed by his inner strength.

" We will hold a service here tonight, Julie. Since the dragoons are gone, we will take the risk. We want to dedicate the young people who are leaving."

Julie remembered the message she had delivered that morning.

Jacques continued, "You will simply do as you're told and join the others when they are called."

Julie's conscience troubled her again. "Father, what if I didn't show up Thursday morning for the departure. If you and I disappeared that day and we went away together, wouldn't everyone here think we had left with the others?" This was Julie's plan, the one her father must accept.

Jacques turned his unseeing eyes away from the fireplace and directly faced Julie. He spoke sternly, "I do not want to hear any more nonsense about this, Julie. It has been decided that you will go. There is no other way." He stood suddenly and slammed his fist upon the table. "None!"

Julie answered slowly and deliberately, "I don't want to go."

Her father's face crumpled as he recognized his own stubbornness in her young voice. "None of our people has defied me in such an important matter. Must revolt come through my own daughter?"

His agony overwhelmed her. Throwing her arms around his neck, she sobbed, "Oh Father, I love you so!" Taking her embrace as submission he said, "There now, that's more like my girl." She lacked the heart to argue further.

Julie was sitting outside on a stump in the shadows when the people began to arrive. They glided into the grove with no sound and hardly any motion. Leaves suddenly rustled and brushed against her arm: a shadowy form lurked in the lilac bushes near the house.

Alarmed, she eased herself away from the bush, knowing a spy could doom their plan and imperil them all. She reached the door of the house as Jacques, leaning heavily on Doctor Boulard's arm, emerged.

"Father," she whispered urgently. "Someone is hiding in the lilac bushes."

"Only friends are here tonight, Julie."

She persisted. "This is an outsider. Why should he hide if he's a friend? Look, he's in the bush, Doctor!"

The doctor agreed. "We must be sure, Jacques."

"Very well, lead me to the bush, and I'll make him identify himself. Julie, you stay here." The two men approached the bush, paused briefly, and returned.

"It's all right, Julie," said Jacques. Doctor Boulard looked at her and shrugged his shoulders. Was he in the dark about the stranger's identity, too?

Auguste appeared with a bag over his shoulder. He grinned at Julie and said, "Take me to the kitchen, Joel." She led him through the door. When they reached the kitchen, Auguste dumped out the contents of his bag, four plump pheasants.

"Auguste, thank you. How good of you to bring such treats for Father."

Auguste winced. "Not just for your father," he declared. "For you, Mademoiselle."

Embarrassed by his attentions, she turned and hurried out the door, closely followed by Auguste. She rushed ahead until they reached the edge of the crowd. Jacques stood in front of the semicircle of cloaked, phantom-like people.

Suddenly, out of the silence a sound arose, so soft and eerie that at first she doubted her ears. She recognized the psalm from her childhood, but had never felt its power as deeply as she did here beneath the stars in the clear sky. Tears filled her eyes as the music rose softly around her.

As Jacques called the names of the children and young people, they came forward, one by one, to kneel before him. When he called the name Joel Brunet, Julie was slow to respond. She was too absorbed in the strange scene. With a start, she hurried forward to kneel in front of her father. She had counted only fourteen names, yet no more were called. Who would be their leader? Was he among the fourteen? Could it be Auguste?

With divided attention, Julie heard only a part of the words her father was speaking to his people. She knew he was reciting words from the Bible – Matthew, she thought he said. She heard him talk about the friends of Jesus meeting him on a mountain where "they worshipped him, but some doubted."

As Jacques continued, she thought about doubters. She contrasted Auguste, a worshipper, with Philippe, a doubter. As for herself, she felt unaccountably left out. She realized she knew too little about her father's religion to even be a doubter.

Jacques' next words captured her wandering attention: something about "go" and then, "Lo, I am with you always, even unto the end of the world." These words from the Book seemed spoken just for them, to encourage these young, defenseless Huguenots, who were really about to "go."

Now she listened, fascinated by Jacques' voice suddenly so penetrating and authoritative that it became unfamiliar to her. "The men to whom Jesus was speaking were as poor, down-trodden, and persecuted as we followers are today. They, too, were a despised minority. But they had a secret which their enemies couldn't understand."

Julie caught her breath. She wanted to know the secret that made her father so courageous and content in spite of the tragedies fate had dealt him.

"They, like we, and like our children who kneel before us and before God, had a constant Companion who is the Son of God Himself!"

Julie's spirits dropped. She was bitterly disappointed. Instead of a secret, Jacques had merely repeated an impossibility. How could he say God was the companion and protector of a people who were killed, dragged dead in streets, blinded and tormented, driven from their homes and families?

When Jacques prayed, Julie's puzzled disappointment prevented her from hearing all the words. She knew that Jacques had literally turned the group over to their God as though he had no doubt that their safety was secure. Was number fifteen supposed to be God, she wondered, then sheepishly shuddered at such a foolish thought. She felt she would never understand this strange, bewildering religion.

The crowd melted away as silently as they had gathered. She took special note that the lilac bush, too, was empty.

News about the marquis had spread among the people. She heard Monsieur Lafaud ask her father, "Why is that evil man coming to our village? It means trouble for us all, we can count on that."

"It won't matter so much after the children get away safely," the doctor said.

When Jacques came into the house, he refused to let her fix him a hot drink. He sent her upstairs to sleep in Lucienne's room. She heard him bolt his door when he entered his tapestry room. Had he dismissed her so definitively to work the secret tapestry or to receive the night visitor?

She paused on the stairs as she heard him coughing. His coughing spells were frequent and violent. She entered the bedroom and asked, "Lucie, what happened to those men Father was telling about, the ones who were told to 'go'?"

Lucienne, who was fluffing the feather bed, paused. Then her puzzled frown cleared as she answered, "Most of them were killed for talking about Jesus, I think."

"Then Jesus let them down, didn't He? They were failures." Julie plopped down upon the soft bed.

"Failures!" exclaimed the woman. "How do you s'pose we'd know about Jesus today if those men were failures? They did go, and they did what they were told to do. They didn't mind death."

Julie remembered the gruesome carvings that represented death in magnificent cathedrals – carvings of monsters, of human agony, of violent deaths of saints. "Are you afraid to die, Lucie?" she asked timidly.

Lucienne walked to the bedside and sat down. Taking her hand as though she was a little girl in the dark again, she said, "I don't want to die, Ma Petite, but I'm not afraid. Death is the best thing that happens to a Christian."

Her eyes widened, and she stared back at Lucienne.

"We go straight to be with the One we trust," Lucienne added.

"You and Father talk about Him as though He were really a live person," said Julie.

"He is a live person to us, Ma Petite. I thought He was to you, too." Her eyes were sorrowful. Julie wanted those kind eyes to sparkle with happiness again.

"Well, maybe He is," she said, ready to end the conversation. She rolled over onto her stomach, and Lucienne took the candle and left quietly for the kitchen where she was to sleep. Julie fell asleep before she could figure out any of the puzzles that haunted her.

At dawn, an agonized cry woke her. "Ma'am'selle! Ma'am'selle! Come quick, it's the master!"

Julie rushed down the stairs and flung herself into her father's room. Lucienne stood wringing her hands, wailing softly. Julie saw by candlelight that her father was still breathing. Blood stained his pillow. Flecks of blood spotted his face and lips.

With great effort, he spoke, "Don't panic, Lucienne." His voice was feeble. "Go find Doc." Julie had already decided to "go find Doc" before she heard these words. She bent to kiss her father tenderly, and she rushed out of the house into the village. As she approached the square, she noticed a commotion unusual at such an early hour A man slumped against the wall of the side street drew her attention. He was in deep distress, groaning, leaning his head against the wall. Occasionally he would raise his head and pound his fists on the stone wall.

"Doctor Boulard, whatever is the matter?"

He turned his stricken face toward Julie. At first, he was speechless. Waving toward the square, he moaned, "Everything is lost, everything! Oh, give me strength!" He leaned once more against the wall.

Julie was truly alarmed. Shaking his arm, she demanded, "What are you talking about? Tell me!"

"They took my children, the intendant and his men. They woke us before daybreak, and only God knows how many others they will steal. I'm wild with anger and frustration, but for the sake of the others, I must control myself!"

Had someone betrayed their plans?

"Father is deathly ill, Doctor. Please go to him, and I will find out all I can about the children." She gently pushed him toward her home, and he stumbled away.

She ran into the square where confusion reigned. She didn't see the Boulard twins, but she saw Madame Lafaud's frantic attempts to tear her two youngest sons from a tall man's grip. As he threw the mother back, her husband tried to calm her.

Auguste bounded from the blacksmith's house, still fastening on his clothes. He tore into the midst of the commotion and demanded, "What are you trying to do with those children?"

"These children have decided to leave their parents and become good Catholics," sneered the tall man who was in charge.

"I don't believe it!" exclaimed Auguste. "I want to ask them!"

At a signal from the tall man, one of his two companions drew a sword. The people gasped as he held it across the throat of Monsieur

Lafaud. The tall man, with an evil grin, turned to the terrified children, whose eyes were fixed on the sword. "Well, children, you don't want to upset anybody, do you? Tell all these people that you want to go along with us."

Monsieur Lafaud started to speak but the soldier pressed the sword against the skin of his throat. The little boys were mute with fear, but they both nodded their heads.

As the man sheathed his sword, Auguste unleashed his fury. "Why you dirty swine! Picking on little kids like this! You ..." His other words were lost as he spun into the uniformed trio.

The three men overpowered the impulsive youth. While one man pinned his arms back and held him, the others gave him a few vicious blows. Then they marched off with the children.

Screaming defiance, Auguste shook both fists after them. "That's your way, take our babies! You're afraid to pick on the big boys. Just wait, someday I'll convert this whole country when I become a pastor of Huguenots like our Jacques de Mirovar!"

Julie had overlooked the carriage parked across the square until the drawn curtains parted and the face of the all-powerful intendant peered out.

"Luc!" His voice stopped the tall leader abruptly. "Go back and get that loud mouth over there. We won't overlook any potential heretic leaders."

The crowd protested as the intendant's men dragged away Auguste, but no one dared interfere. Julie realized that the doctor's supreme efforts at self-control stemmed from wisdom, not cowardice. Only the impulsive Auguste would risk his life, needlessly, against such hopeless odds.

The words of the intendant kept ringing in Julie's ears, "potential heretic leaders." As she followed the captors and captives up the street, her conviction grew that Auguste must be the person that

Jacques had chosen to lead the escape. True, his impulsiveness was a handicap, but his strength and courage were unquestionable. Besides, who else in the group was capable?

Another thought spurred her to closely trail the marching prisoners. If Auguste was the leader, he must not be lost. Julie knew that Jacques was too weak to formulate new plans. She and Jacques must stay behind, but for his sake, she must see that nothing blocked the success of his desperate dream.

Just as she suspected, the intendant's men took the road to the monastery. Julie remained out of sight as they entered the gates. Obviously, the intendant planned this anti-heretic spectacle to impress the marquis and the abbot. Since she had seen no dragoons, only the intendant's men, she surmised that the visitors had not yet arrived.

She ran home as fast as she could. Doctor Boulard met her outside the door and said, "Julie, I didn't tell him about the children. I see no need to distress him further."

She then remembered how much she had upset her father last night by insisting that she remain in Aubusson and by telling him the news of the marquis' arrival. "Could shocking news have brought on this spell?" she asked, fearfully.

"He had to know about the marquis. It could have triggered his attack, but I've been expecting this for a long time. I was hoping he would hold out for one more day."

"The intendant's men hauled the children off to the monastery. They took Auguste, too. May I go in now?" The doctor blocked the doorway.

"Of course you may. I'm sorry, I'm not myself this morning."

Julie felt sure there was a flicker of a smile on Jacques' face as she sat down beside his bed. He senses my presence, she thought, lovingly. The doctor bent over her and said, "There's no more I can do here. Let him rest. I must go to my boys' grandparents. I fear they, as well as the Lafauds, will be needing me."

She hated to see him leave but knew he must. She felt sorry for this man who had no wife, no daughter, and now, no sons. She knew he would hide his own sorrow and minister to others in theirs.

While Julie kept vigil by her father, she planned how she might help Auguste escape. She was probably the only one who could enter the monastery, on this day in particular. She didn't want to leave her father, but when he slept, perhaps she could do something.

"Julie."

"Yes, Father."

"Please fetch my Bible."

Julie looked around the room and saw it lying on a table nearby. She found it strange that a blind man still kept his Bible handy. She had seen him take this same Book when he visited his tapestry weavers in the old days, reading and praying with even the lowliest weavers in the scattered little cottages or hovels. She had often tagged along, but these trips had usually bored her.

When she sat down again, he told her, "I want you to have this Book, Julie."

"Thank you, Father."

"I don't think you realize it's not just a book, it is a living Book. It speaks to you like a friend if you will let it. It's company when you're lonely and it holds the answer to all of life's problems. Will you promise to give it a chance?"

"Yes, Father."

"You will take it with you tomorrow?"

She hesitated. She decided she didn't have to tell him where she would take it tomorrow. "All right, Father."

After a moment of silence, he spoke again. "Read to me."

She opened the Book, not knowing where to start. Since it opened to the Psalms, she began reading there. She became absorbed in the lyrical words of the psalmist who had also escaped enemies, faced death, but always trusted God.

Recognizing a deep stillness, she looked up. With a soft cry, she touched her father's forehead. She felt his wrist. She knew that the relaxation of his pained facial muscles was permanent – her father was dead!

Lucienne came out of the shadows and put an arm around her. They knelt beside the bed and sobbed for a few moments, but then Julie sprang to her feet. She remembered the dragoons dragging the old man through the village.

"Lucie, there is no time to grieve. We must ... bury him!" She choked over the words.

Lucienne objected, saying, "No, we must have a service. We can't just bury him like a dog!"

"Remember Dominique?" From the expression on Lucienne's terrified face, she did. "Well, what do you suppose they will do to Father if they find out? There is no time to send for anyone, and it would be dangerous if we did. We can have the service, you and I, if that will make you feel better."

Lucienne cooperated in a daze. She told Julie that Jacques had asked his friends to bury him at the far end of the grove. Julie was glad some of his friends would remember his request.

With Lucienne's help, she performed the necessary functions as if in a nightmare. They wrapped his body in the gray cloth that he had kept over the mysterious tapestry, which was now gone. "I wish we could wrap him in a beautiful tapestry," Julie sighed.

"They're all gone," sobbed Lucienne. The tapestries had been taken away the night before to be prepared for their trip to the fair.

Early morning sunlight filtered through the trees as Julie dug the trench for her father's body. It was hard work, and sad, but she didn't stop to pity herself. Time was precious and danger very real. As her final service to her father, she resolved not to linger in grief over his body, but to fulfill his wishes among the living. So, he would have his way after all. She would bear his blood and his ideals into the New World.

They respectfully carried his body out of the house and lowered it into the grave. Julie read the twenty-third Psalm, which she had read to Jacques earlier. She thought the passage fit, for it promised God's companionship through the "valley of the shadow of death." Brushing her tears away, she signaled to Lucienne to start filling the grave.

Even before the earth covered her father's body, Julie began to give instructions. "Lucie, you must start immediately for your kinfolk in the Auvergne. You will be in great danger when his absence is noted."

Lucienne put down the stick she had been using and sobbed, "My work is over. There's no matter what happens to me."

"Must I leave Aubusson, worrying about your safety?"

At these words, Lucienne stood up with a determined look on her face. "All right, Ma Petite, we won't meet again in this world, but we will on the other side."

It took Julie a moment to interpret her meaning, and then she hugged her tightly. Thrusting Jacques' Bible into her smock, she said, "I'm going back by the house while you smooth this over. Don't forget to hide all signs of the burial. Goodbye, dearest Lucie!"

Julie hurried into the house and picked up Auguste's pheasants that no one had had time to prepare. She took a last look around her home, choking down the sobs that tore at her chest. She closed the door behind her softly. Then she took a short cut to the chateau and was soon ringing for admittance to the monastery.

Chapter XV
The Marquis Comes

"Good day," smiled the old man as he opened the gate. Julie slipped past him with a word of greeting and walked briskly to the kitchen door. In answer to her question, a young novitiate who was carrying water into the kitchen pointed out the superior prior.

The prior, the highest ranking monk in the monastery, didn't seem to have aged. Julie remembered his kind eyes, his uncommonly white face rising above his black habit, and the little square black cap on top his bald head. Today his expression was tense and harassed. Holding out her offering to him, she stammered, "I brought these birds to you."

The prior turned from the novitiate he was scolding. "Very good." He spoke as if accustomed to gifts from the faithful. "You brought them at a good time if these slow fools can get around to fixing them."

"I'll clean them for you," Julie offered.

The surprised prior looked intently at her. "Who are you, boy? Have I seen you around?"

"Likely. I'm a local apprentice," said Julie. With a flourish, she pulled Albert's hunting knife from its usual spot in her smock pocket and strode out the door.

As she sat on the wood block near the kitchen door clumsily plucking the pheasants, she silently thanked Lucienne for recently training her in kitchen work. Valjean had not prepared her for this task. A novitiate brought her a basket of onions to peel and cut. She took the entrails from the pheasants and personally fed them to the dogs, carefully protecting her hands from their eager mouths. She wanted these dogs to be her friends.

She heard a clatter and a loud halloo outside the gates. The old man fumbled in his haste to open the gates to the horsemen who waited noisily outside. Julie hurried back to the onions and absorbed herself in her task.

From the corner of her eyes she watched two great, handsome horses arrive carrying splendidly dressed riders. She immediately recognized the marquis, who appeared travel-worn and dusty. His companion wore an elegant red cloak over black silk vestments. Gloves of richly embroidered linen covered his hands, and a magnificent sapphire ring adorned one finger. He obviously was the powerful church official, the Abbot de Clugny, whom she had seen leading holy processions in Paris. She understood why the monks were so impressed and excited.

The intendant's carriage rolled into the court behind the guests' prancing horses. The intendant, who had met the guests at the edge of the village, descended. It seemed to Julie that a whole regiment of dragoons and colorful attendants stood in the background. She recognized Lafayere and his men. She hoped the dragoons wouldn't return to the tapissier today. This risk she had overlooked.

Suddenly the marquis wheeled his horse around, and Julie ducked her head to avoid his eyes. The marquis was angry, and the whole company acted disturbed and confused.

"I must say, when the king's men and the Church's servants cannot ride in safety through the countryside, things have come to a poor pass," sputtered the marquis to the intendant. "These renegades were so bold as to attack even our large armed group. Although we wounded two of them, they stole five of our horses and escaped. It's scandalous! The king will be very displeased when I report this to him."

The intendant tried to soothe the guest. "We've been hunting these men for several days. We will send the soldiers back out immediately, now that they've brought you here safely. If you will leave your horses here, they will be cared for while you accompany me to my quarters for lunch. This is not Paris, but we shall do our best for our distinguished guests." He bowed slightly to each man.

"Don't be offended, Monsieur, but I prefer to stay here and rest," responded the abbot. He looked sick.

"As you like, Your Reverence," agreed the intendant.

The marquis was still fuming as he dismounted. "Between the renegades and the Huguenots, this country is rather spoiled, isn't it, Monsieur Bregal? What are you doing about it?"

"We're doing all we can. Only this morning, we rounded up several children who have agreed to come into the Mother Church and forsake the heresies of their parents," Monsieur Bregal replied.

"Children, children! Is that all you can find to bring to justice?" demanded the marquis. "Perhaps I shall want to see these children," he added, thoughtfully.

"Certainly, tonight, when we dine here," said the intendant.

Some novitiates led the horses away. The soldiers received orders from the intendant and left. The marquis and the abbot stood talking in low tones not far from Julie. As the marquis strode directly toward Julie, her heart skipped a beat. She kept her face tilted downwards and her shaking hands busy with the onions.

He stopped so close to her, she could feel his warm breath on her skin but he never looked into her eyes. He reached into her basket, took an onion, grasped her knife, and made a gash that removed the outer skins. He placed the knife back in her hand. As she heard his teeth bite into the raw, crisp onion, she sighed with relief.

"How can you eat an onion after that miserable ride this morning?" the abbot asked, walking over to stand beside the marquis.

"Onions are good for the stomach. You should try one," laughed the marquis with his mouth full. The intendant called to him, and he strode to the carriage. Julie still did not lift her head. The abbot had not moved away.

"You've cut your hand, Child." His voice was strange and hollow. "Your beautiful hands fascinate me."

Julie didn't reply. She wondered if she should bow in his presence or continue her work. She wished he would leave quickly.

Monks hovered at a respectful distance. The prior seemed uncertain whether to interrupt or not. Julie jumped slightly as the abbot's hand cupped under her chin.

"Why don't you look up, boy? Are you afraid?" he asked, forcing her head up. Her eyes were full of tears caused by the onions. The abbot smiled kindly, but the absolute power and unquestioned authority in his face awed Julie. Why should this important stranger be interested in an humble servant boy?

At last, the abbot responded to the reverent honor the monks and novitiates offered. They led him inside the monastery, and Julie sighed with relief.

A novitiate stood at her elbow looking at her with respect in his blue eyes. "Madame Pantier didn't bring the eggs she promised this morning. Go to her cottage and tell her the prior must have all her eggs. Bring them back with you."

She relished an excuse to go into town and return without suspicion. The capture of the children undoubtedly stunned the villagers, and they would wonder if the escape was still possible. She hurried into the village, first stopping by the wool merchant's. Monsieur Lafaud looked startled when the bell over the door tinkled.

"Monsieur Lafaud, I'm in a hurry. I want to be sure that everyone follows our plans for tomorrow."

Monsieur Lafaud didn't answer and appeared hostile. Julie knew she had spoken too openly, but she knew no secret code names, and she was in a desperate hurry. He obviously didn't trust her.

How could she win his trust? If Auguste and the children escaped tonight, they desperately needed to leave town early tomorrow. Yet she couldn't reveal her plans, for she hadn't completed them.

She spoke as earnestly as she could. "Monsieur Jacques de Mirovar commands that we proceed as planned. We must trust his plan. Do you understand?"

Monsieur Lafaud brightened when Julie mentioned Jacques. "Of course, Jacques will know a way to get the boys out of that place. Yes, we will go ahead. You tell Jacques not to worry about us. We'll have everything ready. He can count on us."

Now Julie realized why no one should find out about Jacques' death. As long as the Huguenots thought he was alive and masterminding the plans, their courage would not waver.

She left the shop and hurried to Madame Pantier's where she fetched the eggs. She started back to the chateau knowing she must not be gone too long.

Half way up the steep hill, she noticed someone following her. His cloaked figure was approaching rapidly. She stopped when she recognized the doctor. He was frowning intensely.

"Where's Jacques? Where's Lucie? Do you know what has happened to them?"

She didn't answer. Her secret sorrow weighed on her like a crushing burden. Doctor Boulard misunderstood her choked silence.

"Did the dragoons take him? Did they? Did they?"

"Oh, no! He ... he didn't recover, Doctor. I know I killed him. Last night I told him I wouldn't leave Aubusson, and that killed him." Julie bent her head as her tears fell.

The doctor put his arm around her shoulders. "I was afraid he hadn't been blessed with a peaceful death," he said. "No, Julie, don't blame yourself for his merciful death. We can be glad he's at peace."

"He died while I was reading his Bible to him," Julie said.

"I'm very glad," he said sincerely. "Where is his body?"

Julie started to tell him. "I mustn't tell you, Doctor, for your own safety, but Lucie and I buried him where he had requested. Then I sent Lucie away. It is done. We had as good a service as we knew how to have."

Boulard took her into his arms for only an instant, lest they be seen. "You've truly grown up, Julie. I know all I need to know. I'm very happy for poor Jacques. No one knew how much he suffered."

"Wait!" cried Julie, as he started to go. "You must not let anyone know about his death."

"No?"

"Everyone thinks he's alive and directing the escape of the children from the chateau."

Doctor Boulard stared at Julie with disbelief. "What do you mean?"

"The children in the chateau will make that rendezvous as planned tomorrow, I promise you. I don't know how yet, but they will be there. Please make sure the townspeople cooperate. Please!"

"Julie! I don't know what you're up to, but God bless you. It would be more sensible for you to get out of town immediately. The marquis hopes to find you in this vicinity, according to his soldiers, but you're too much like your father to run away."

"I owe a debt to my father and to the people of this town who cared for him during all these years. I shall pay it tonight," she said.

"I believe you will. We shall be praying for you in the village. I won't tell about Jacques."

Julie hurried up the hill, pleased that the sad slump of the doctor's shoulders had straightened a little.

As she crossed the church square a few yards outside the chateau gates, she recognized Comrade at the feet of one of the de Vauve servants. She hadn't seen Philippe since yesterday on the bridge, and so much had happened since then. Philippe should know about Jacques' death. Who would tell him?

"Where's your master, Comrade?" she called. The dog ran to greet Julie warmly and wetly. She laughed.

"Comrade is trying to tell you that he's unhappy about his master. The Captain rode to Montlucon, and Comrade thinks he has gone forever," the servant said.

She gave the dog a last pat and went on. The mention of Montlucon brought back memories of her trip with Philippe from the north, their night at Montlucon, and their adventures the next day. She knew she would never see Philippe again. She hoped that the angry, relentless Philippe of that trip would vanish and the gentle friend she had loved as a child would re-emerge.

As she reentered the monastery gates, she knew a crucial drama would take place before she left again. The dangers, increased since the arrival of the marquis and the abbot, failed to suppress the optimism and hope in her heart. Was the Huguenot spirit contagious? Had the mantle of her father figuratively fallen upon her? Why did she not feel alone as she launched her daring hopes and plans?

Julie had no time to ponder these mighty questions, for as soon as she gave the eggs to the novitiate, the monks pressed more jobs upon her. She felt grateful for the work. Since she couldn't have the luxury of mourning her father's death, it was best to avoid thinking of him.

Still, she was glad she had his Bible. She reached her hand into her smock to reassure herself. Her spine tingled. The Book was gone. If she had dropped it within the monastery, she could expect serious trouble if it were found. Where was the Book?

Chapter XVI
The Abbot Makes an Offer

Julie groped her way across the steamy kitchen to an open window. She pushed the damp curls from her forehead and welcomed a light breeze that cooled her perspiring brow. It had been a long, weary time since Lucienne's cry had awakened her that morning. She must not falter now.

She found no trace of the Bible she had dropped. She hoped that it wasn't in the monastery. Although she regretted the loss of this dear reminder of Jacques, she must forget the Book and concentrate on freeing the Huguenot children. She had no idea where the authorities had imprisoned the children.

A bell rang in the distance, calling the monks to vespers. Julie entered a doorway that opened into the cloister. This was an open courtyard surrounded on four sides by a covered walkway where the monks walked for exercise and meditation. She saw the last of the cloaked figures disappear through an arched doorway at the far end of the cloister. She wondered, since the monastery was built around the cloister, if the children might be in one of the many rooms that lined the walkway.

No one noticed her as she slipped into the walkway and paused beside a beautiful fountain where the monks washed before meals. Graceful vines with reddening leaves climbed the slender wooden pillars that supported the cloister roofs. The grassy courtyard, with formal flowerbeds and a half dozen statues of saints, was immaculately kept. Dusk had already reached this quiet, secluded retreat.

Keeping close to the walls, Julie slipped noiselessly along the walkway. The first door that she tried was locked. The next door gave way, and she recognized the infirmary. She found other simple rooms but no trace of the children. She flattened herself against the wall as she heard a noise in the cloister. When nothing appeared, she blamed it on the birds, who were noisily discussing their sleeping arrangements in the colorful vines overhead.

Julie reached the far side of the cloister, where she had guessed the chapel was located, when she found herself face to face with the Abbot de Clugny. He stood in the archway, watching her intently. After an instant of shocked apprehension, she fell to her knees at his feet. Unsure how long he had been spying on her, she dared not look up at his face.

"What are you doing in the cloister?" His voice was stern.

"I ... I was looking for the chapel, Your Grace," she stammered.

His voice softened. "You have found it," he gestured toward the door behind him, "but why should you go to vespers? Don't you belong in the kitchen?"

Julie was amazed that he knew anything about her and was surprised to hear a chuckle in his voice. She didn't answer, wishing she had never left the kitchen.

"I'm glad you came along, boy. I've been asking questions about you. What is your name?"

"Joel, sire."

"Are you a recruit for the monastery?"

"No, sire, I am an extra hand for today, only."

"Who are your parents?"

"I have no parents, sire. I am an apprentice in the village."

"Splendid," he said. When Julie looked up, he was smiling at her. "I've been strangely attracted by you, lad. You seem intelligent and have superior bearing. Your extremely good looks are an advantage.

How would you like to become a page in my court?"

Julie swallowed hard. "Oh, sire, I am very lowly born and very stupid. I could never learn the fancy ways of your grand court."

"I hoped you wouldn't show this lack of ambition I find in most peasants," he sighed. "However, I can help you overcome such indolence. If you obey me, there is no limit to your possibilities – education, wealth, perhaps even a title. All these can be yours, in return for loyalty to me. What think you of that?"

She didn't dare say what she thought of that. In the abbot, she recognized the same signs of power and ambition that marked her uncle and the marquis. Her life would be forfeit if he knew that a mere maid knelt before him, making a fool of him and his schemes.

The abbot patted his cloak. "Truly, Joel, I'm an expert judge of character. I can spot a promising young lad like you in unpromising surroundings and lift him up to become whatever I choose."

"But, sire, I am unworthy. I'm not even pious enough to serve you."

The abbot laughed heartily. "At least you're honest, but we can correct that fault, too."

The prior dashed through the door and stopped, stunned, when he saw the abbot laughing and the servant lad kneeling before him. He looked from one to the other. "Excuse me, Your Grace, is the boy pestering you?"

"On the contrary, my friend, I am indebted to you for finding him for me. He's to accompany me when I leave here."

The prior's eyes wandered over Julie searchingly as he replied, "Of course, Your Grace."

Julie responded gladly to the dismissal gesture that the abbot finally gave her. She hurried directly to the kitchen, shaken from this strange turn of events. She still knew nothing of the children's whereabouts.

As she darted through the kitchen door, she almost collided with a young novitiate whose face was openly curious. That afternoon he had introduced himself to her as Brother John.

"Are you in trouble?" he asked her.

"No, 'course not," she answered.

"Why was the abbot talking to you for so long?"

"He was offering me a job."

"A job? You treat an offer from the Abbot de Clugny like that, as just a job?" He sounded incredulous. "You're a funny one."

Brother John stacked six wooden bowls and spoons on a large tray. He poured weak soup into an earthenware tureen.

"What's that for?" she asked.

"I'm about to feed our prisoners. I understand one of your friends is included," he answered.

Julie's face whitened. Was her connection with the Huguenots known?

"I was in the square the other day when you gave that Huguenot smithy a good dunking. Now he will be taken away for good, and it's just what he deserves."

Julie rubbed the nape of her neck and said, "He's very, very strong, Auguste is. I was lucky he didn't beat me up. I hope they have him in a secure place here."

"I'd like to see him get out of the old chateau dungeon," said Brother John. "The children are there, too."

"That's a good place for that bully," said Julie. "I wish I could see him when he can't lord it over everyone else."

"Why don't you help me carry this soup to them? Luc was going to help me, but he'll be glad to get out of it."

"Certainly." She struggled to hide her elation as she followed him across the cloister and through a door leading to the other side of the chateau grounds. Leaving the monastery buildings behind, they approached the ruins of the old donjon towers. Though the towers lay in ruins, the dungeons, Brother John explained, were intact below ground.

He pulled out a key and opened the outside door. Julie could hear weeping nearby. After they entered, the young monk locked the door, leaving them in total darkness. The stench of the dungeon was stifling. She pitied the children, locked in such a dark, frightening place.

"Wait, while I light a candle," Brother John said, as he placed his tray on the dirt floor. Extending the lighted candle toward Julie, he said, "Carry it."

"You'll have to put it into my hand," she answered, for she needed both her hands to carry the bread and the water jug.

"What a place for children," she added.

"It was the only safe place we could put them. The intendant made his move before we were ready for them, just to impress our guests. We'll get the children out and send them to Limoges tomorrow or the next day, when we have others to send with them."

Brother John set his tray down again in order to lift the latch on a second door. After they passed through, Julie saw the three little Boulard boys and the two Lafaud children huddled together in a far corner. As the smallest Boulard whimpered, his brother, Zachary, held him tightly. Thomas jumped forward, defiantly, as though to shield his brothers. His unconcealed contempt for Julie pained her, but she pretended indifference.

As they gave the children the food, Brother John sighed, wrinkling his nose with distaste as he said, "We have to wait until they finish, you know."

"Feed Auguste, too – he's in there," said Zachary, as he ate the lukewarm soup hungrily. Julie guessed correctly that this was their first meal since their incarceration.

"Give us time, Minion. Joel, you'd best help me – be careful."

She unlocked the door and swung it open. Auguste sat on the dirt floor, his feet and hands bound with ropes.

"How is he going to eat?" exclaimed Brother John, plainly exasperated, but making no move to untie Auguste. He shook his head vigorously when Julie suggested releasing his hands.

"Then we'll have to feed him." She tried to appear as anxious to leave the nasty place as the young monk. "Shall I do it?"

"If he'll let you." Brother John turned away from the hateful, fierce expression on the captive youth's face.

Auguste briefly showed astonishment upon seeing Julie. She wasn't sure whether he believed she was here to help or because she was on the enemy's side. She knelt beside him and began to feed him with shaking hands. She was silent, though she yearned to warn him to eat well because he would need all his strength tonight.

She called to Brother John, "Do you suppose these children will be brought before the marquis tonight looking like this?"

"They are filthy and disheveled, aren't they," he replied. Julie didn't really care how they looked, she just wanted Auguste to understand that he would leave this place, briefly, this evening.

Her companion stepped into the other room to take a bowl from a child. Quickly, Julie slipped the hunting knife that she had used in the kitchen all afternoon into Auguste's hands behind him. "Wait until after ... marquis." She dared whisper no more, hoping that he understood that he must not use the knife until after his appearance before the marquis.

Julie no longer doubted Auguste trusted her. He whined, "Not much here to satisfy a body that's gone hungry all day. I'm so starved I could eat those bones."

She noticed his emphasis on the last word and threw the tiny poultry bones from the empty bowl onto the dirt floor near his feet.

"There, you dog! There's your bones, that's all you deserved in the first place."

Brother John locked every door, checking each carefully before they left. Back in the kitchen, another monk told Julie that she was expected to spend the night at the monastery.

"With all the extra company, I can't see how we can put you up, too," he grumbled. "You can't stay in the dormitory because you haven't taken the vows."

"What about the hayloft?" Julie smiled wryly, as her words reminded her of Philippe.

"Yes, that is the answer, but don't say we made you sleep there, please. Say you asked to, if anybody questions you."

Julie heard the commotion when the guests arrived, but the confusion and clatter in the kitchen kept her from hearing what transpired in the dining room. She rushed about, hauling water, receiving empty platters, rinsing the mountains of dishes the diners were using.

Work slacked off, and Julie sought a corner where she could rest her tired feet. Brother John stopped her, saying, "They've sent for the children. This should be fun."

She wished that the children could avoid the ordeal of being entertainment for the drunken men. She followed Brother John into the cloister to observe the revelry of the distinguished company through the open doors and windows.

The intendant and the marquis wasted little time on the younger children, who were tired and frightened, offering little sport for the diners. The strapping blacksmith was more interesting.

The intendant questioned Auguste about Huguenot activities, but his answers were so evasive that the intendant lost patience. "I heard your outburst in the public square today. Did you not declare yourself one of them?"

Auguste lifted his head, looked his questioner in the eye, and declared, "I did, sir. I am a Huguenot."

"Then answer me these questions. Is not Jacques Mirovar your leader? Is he not planning a treasonable action against the king?"

Auguste's voice was steady and clear. "I am a Huguenot, but I cannot answer those questions."

"You mean, you will not!" The intendant's voice squeaked with fury. He slapped Auguste across his cheek. Auguste's bound arms bulged as he automatically reacted to this attack. When the intendant ordered the youth removed to receive a whipping, the marquis interceded.

"Wait! I would like to question this young man, also." The intendant reluctantly backed away, glancing at the abbot who observed everything silently.

"What is your age?" the marquis asked him.

"Nineteen."

"Uh-huh, so I guessed. How long have you lived in Aubusson?"

"All my life."

"In that case, whether you admit it or not, you're acquainted with Jacques Mirovar, de Mirovar, I believe his friends still insist on calling him. Since this is true, you have known his daughter, yes?" When Auguste didn't answer, the marquis persisted, "As a little girl, perhaps?"

"Yes. I knew her long ago before she went away."

The marquis smiled confidently. "But now that she's back, you don't know her?"

Auguste did not fall for this. "If she is back, Jacques de Mirovar hides his daughter well."

"No doubt, no doubt! Perhaps not even all the villagers know she is back, no? But something tells me you do know, or you could find out if you so desired." Leaning forward, he hissed, "I will make it worth your efforts, Auguste Craone. You will be set free, even sent abroad with money in your pocket, if that is what you want."

Auguste moistened his lips. "I believe that Jacques de Mirovar would never tell me the location of his daughter, even if she was in Aubusson," he said.

"But I can see that the idea is beginning to appeal to you." The marquis turned to the intendant. "Send this youth back to his cell with no beating, and I shall continue my discussion with him tomorrow after he's had a night in bonds to think about my offer."

The intendant signaled the guards to take the children away. Julie was certain Auguste would never betray her, but he had been offered a tempting reward. She doubted the marquis would honor any promises he made to Auguste, but the youth didn't know that.

Rain was falling lightly when Julie left the kitchen for the hayloft. She was glad she didn't have to figure out a way to reenter the chateau grounds, since she was to spend the night here. As she climbed the ladder inside the stable, she noticed that it leaned against a wall of the old stableman's room. Also, the dogs were sleeping in the stable because of the rainstorm. If she descended the ladder later tonight, she would have to face these challenges.

When she reached the top of the ladder, she held high the tiny lamp that Brother John had loaned her and looked anxiously around. There was a large opening at the back of the loft. She went to this window and looked out, barely recognizing, in the dim lamp light, an old wagon below.

She extinguished the lamp and sat down near the window. She waited until the monastery had been quiet for a long time before she moved. Then, as softly as a shadow, she lowered herself from the window onto the wagon seat. No dogs came out to investigate. She crept across the yard toward the dungeon. She wished she could have gotten the keys to open the doors, but she did not come away empty handed. She pulled a meat cleaver from the waistband beneath her smock when she reached the door to the dungeon. She saw immediately that she couldn't use the cleaver on the heavy, solid door. The noise would arouse the monastery.

Julie ran her hands along the door, studying it with her fingers. Suddenly a bolt of lightening startled her, and when a crash of thunder followed, she threw herself against the wall.

Huge drops of rain pelted her. She wished the storm had held off for a few hours until she realized the weather would help her. The noise of the storm would drown out any sounds they made, the dogs wouldn't prowl the premises, and everyone would stay in their snug beds. With new courage, she turned again to the formidable door.

Chapter XVII
Escape From a Dungeon

The rain water dripped from Julie's hair, running down her face and neck. She shivered from cold and from desperation. The time, she judged, was well past midnight and she was no closer to rescuing the children.

She tried to force open the door with the meat cleaver, but this was fruitless. Staring forlornly at the heavy oak door, she fought back her feeling of despair. She had to find a way. She bent her head to the door and listened, for she thought she heard a noise from the other side. She knocked sharply three times and stifled a cry of joy when three knocks sounded from beyond. With new courage, she forced the meat cleaver into the door crack once more, trying to contact the lock. Then she remembered the dirt floor. Stooping, she felt beneath the door, but the space there was very narrow. With a few blows and digs, she made a larger opening.

"Down here, Auguste, I'm digging under the door," she called through the small space. "Help me!"

Digging hurriedly, impatient with her slow progress, she suddenly felt her tool pulled roughly from her hands. After a pang of fear, she realized that hands from under the door had grabbed the tool. Of course, strong Auguste would make the hole larger more easily and quickly than she. She helped dig with her hands until the space was large enough for a child to squeeze through.

One by one, the five little boys slipped under the door. Julie hugged each one and shoved each gently against the wall with a warning, "Shhh, not a sound! We must not arouse the dogs."

After more digging, Auguste squeezed through the hole. He reached out for Julie and pulled her close to him, neither of them daring to speak. She rested in the comforting strength of his arms only briefly, then drew back, whispering, "We must not waken the dogs but we must hurry. Follow me."

Auguste apparently knew the chateau ruins, too. Together they guided the children to a big, gnarled apple tree that grew beyond the towers. The children sensed their urgency and cooperated like veteran adventurers.

"Auguste, you go first, up the tree and over the wall. Coax the children to jump to you on the other side," Julie whispered.

He patted each boy on the shoulder. "Hold tight and climb like a squirrel. If you slip and fall, you'll spoil everything."

Julie remembered her own childhood escapades in this tree. Branches started low to the ground and rose making a sturdy ladder a child could easily climb. The main dangers were the slippery wet bark and the dark of the night.

A hard thump on the other side of the wall assured her that Auguste had landed. Little Matt Boulard was first to climb the tree. She held her breath, listening to his movements. Against the dark sky, she could see his tiny form dimly silhouetted on the wall before he disappeared over the side. The two Lafaud boys followed without mishap, then Zachary.

As Thomas was mounting the tree, one of the big dogs came bounding through the darkness. The charging dog so frightened him that he missed a limb and fell about four feet to the ground. Without hesitating, Julie threw herself in front of the dog as he rushed toward the boy.

"Up that tree, quick!" she cried to the terrified Thomas, who shot up the tree like lightening. The barking dog circled the tree, surprised by Julie's sudden action. She turned all her attention upon the dog.

"There, now," she soothed her voice. "Don't you remember me? Remember all that good food I gave you this afternoon?"

Hesitating only a moment, the dog started toward Julie, still barking. If she didn't hush him, the other dogs would soon join in and arouse everyone.

Then a tiny, dark form came hurtling over the wall, landing in motion just beyond her. The dog dashed after the running shape, and Julie sprinted up the tree.

"That poor cat," she said, as she landed beside Auguste on the other side. "I hope he can run fast, as fast as you were thinking when you threw him over the wall."

"Don't waste your concern on that cat," said Auguste. "He's a terror. He can outsmart that whole pack of dogs."

"What, now?" Julie turned naturally to him now, as leader.

"It would be safer to take the boys directly to the rendezvous place outside the village, but then they couldn't say goodbye to their families. Don't you think we should take them home first?" Auguste needed help with this decision.

"Is there time?"

"Plenty. The tapestry cart won't leave until a half hour before sunrise," he replied. Then he added, ruefully, brushing the water off his shoulders, "That is, when the sun ought to rise."

"Then let's go to the village," said Julie.

The lightening had abated but the rain still came down in torrents. The muddy streets had become small rivers, through which the silent party sloshed on their way to Doctor Boulard's house, their first stop.

Auguste's soft knock was answered quickly. Dr. Boulard opened the door, swept them all inside, and called out as though he expected them, "They're here!" The room was full of people. The children tumbled into the arms of joyful, weeping adults, while Julie looked around, amazed.

"We have been praying for you youngsters all night," said the doctor. "I told you we would do our part, Ju … Joel!"

Auguste told them how they escaped, and Julie learned how, after freeing his hands, he used the chicken bones to stuff the lock before the key was turned in his cell door. As the parents cuddled lovingly with their children savoring their last moments with them, Julie slipped into the passageway her eyes spilling over with tears. Memories of her father's death hit her with full force as she sorrowfully witnessed this scene of anxious, loving families. She felt so alone.

Auguste found Julie in the hall and touched her arm, saying, "Do you want me to go to Monsieur Jacques with you?"

"No, no!" she said with such intensity that he looked at her, puzzled. "There isn't time," she added, spreading out her hands.

"Of course there is, just time enough to slip in and then get going," He started to open the door.

When she didn't move, he closed the door and looked into her face. With one rough finger, he touched a tear that was creeping down her cheek. "What is it, dear Julie, tell me! I can't bear to see you cry."

She shook her head and didn't answer. He took her by the shoulders, looking deep into her eyes. "Has something happened to Monsieur Jacques?" The anger in his face reminded her of Doctor Boulard's first thought of violence toward her father.

"No, not that, Auguste, they didn't get him. It's …"

"But he's gone, isn't he," Auguste persisted.

Julie nodded. Auguste's face crumpled in intense grief before he turned away from her. After a moment of silence, he said, "He was the same as my father, too, you know. He was father to all of us. Our shepherd! Blind Jacques could see more clearly than the rest of us could see with eyes."

Julie nodded, crying silently.

"Julie, a man like Jacques does not die. Wherever I go, he'll be my inspiration. I want my life to be like his – in the New World."

Julie was thinking of his reference to her father as a shepherd, remembering that Lucienne had said that, too. What an appropriate description of him. She wiped her tears and smiled. "You're right, Auguste, we won't think of Jacques as dead. We'll let him lead us right out of this tormented country to a land of freedom."

He lifted her hand, kissing it softly. She turned her face away from his searching eyes that showed so plainly his tenderness toward her.

As Auguste started back into the crowded room, Julie laid her hand upon his arm. "Please, don't mention Jacques' death to them. They have enough sorrow of their own. Doc knows, and he will tell them, later." He nodded and gently squeezed her hand.

He reentered the room, saying, "Give me half an hour to get over the city wall. Does everyone know the place and time each child is to cross the wall? Good, then I will be ready to receive them, one by one, according to plan. We must be far away from Aubusson before we're missed."

As Auguste turned around, his eyes met Julie's. "All is Jacques' planning; we're simply carrying it out," he explained. She followed him across the room, where he stopped to speak to the Lafauds, who were putting on their cloaks. "Let Joel go home with you. Since I'm supposedly locked up at the chateau, only Jeanne, Didier, and Joel will leave with the cart from the South Gate. Proceed due south until you reach the road forking toward Limoges. Then turn west and keep going until you reach the Brown Mill, where we will be waiting for you."

Julie went home with Jeanne and Didier. The Lafaud parents escorted their three younger sons to the city wall and watched them climb safely out of Aubusson. By the clock on the mantle of the wool shop, there was time for two hours sleep, but no one felt like sleeping. They hovered over the fire and talked little, waiting anxiously for the Lafaud parents to return and say that all was well.

Julie was dozing when Monsieur and Madame Lafaud returned. They reassured the young people, "Everything went off as planned, as far as we know."

"The storm is over," added his wife in a flat voice.

"We'd better check the tapestry cart," Didier fidgeted. "Isn't it almost time?"

"And we must finish the lunches," said Jeanne. She and her mother began wrapping cheese, bread, water bottles, and dried fruit. They would take a copious supply of food.

Finally, it was time to go to the cart, though there was barely a glow in the eastern sky. Food was deposited among the tapestries, which were carefully covered with a coarse canvas. Didier hitched his father's only remaining mule to the cart. His father watched with moist eyes knowing he would never see his son again, never see him grow into manhood, but also knowing he would never see him bound in chains or spat upon or dragged through the streets and called a dog. His father knew his son left for a better life and struggled to hold back his tears to ease the pain of parting.

Didier and Jeanne's mother was less silent. "Oh, children – now make sure you don't go out in the cold barefoot, and eat plenty of green vegetables and, oh, oh, I'm so happy you're going, and I love you so and … and … I'll miss you so!" She sobbed softly as she hugged her fidgety son and anxious daughter.

"And Jeanne, Jeanne, take good care of my babies, dear!" Julie heard the distraught mother's plea as she clung to her daughter, "You must be mother to all the children. God bless and keep every one of you."

The mule plodded slowly down the muddy street, pulling the heavy cart toward the south gate. Jeanne rode on top the cart while Julie and Didier walked. Julie sidestepped the deeper mud holes as she trudged along the road, now a slimy stream. The Creuse River threatened to overflow its banks. Ahead loomed the closed gate of the town.

A sleepy guard first checked his orders, then opened the gate without questioning. As the cart passed through, Julie fought back tears; she knew she was leaving her home, her childhood, her father – forever. Though Julie was tired and groggy from lack of sleep, her spirits lifted as they left the gate behind them. A glance at the chateau on the hilltop revealed no hint of the previous night's adventures there.

Didier shouted at the mule and poked his hide with a pointed stick, but failed to induce the mule to pick up his lazy pace. Didier was losing patience.

"Let me try for awhile," suggested Julie. Taking the animal's bridle in hand, she trudged alongside the mule, coaxing him in a gentle, constant voice. The mud clung to her legs, as she slipped and slid, but the mule's pace was noticeably quicker.

"Must we keep this beast all the way?" complained Jeanne, who sat safely out of the mud on top of the cart.

"I don't know, but we'll never make La Rochelle if we have to drag along like this all the way." Didier replied.

The road left the river and approached a steep hill. The mule balked. Julie coaxed and Didier scolded. Didier brought his heavy stick down hard upon the mule's back, but he moved only a few inches before stopping again.

Turning to Jeanne, Didier yelled, "Get off that wagon and help us!"

"But, Didier, I'll get all muddy," she wailed.

"You'll get worse 'n that if we don't get movin'. If me and Joel can wade through muck, so can you ...," his voice softened, as he added, "That is, so long as we need you bad, like right now."

"But you're boys," said Jeanne, climbing down from the cart. Julie noticed that, except for a useless effort to protect her long skirts, Jeanne pushed as industriously as her brother. Finally, they reached the top of the hill and started down.

A quarter of a mile ahead, Julie saw the Brown Mill. "Look, who is that with Auguste?" She pointed down the hill at a man on horseback.

"I don't know, but I don't like it. Auguste seems to be arguing with him," Didier exclaimed.

"I don't see the children," Jeanne noted anxiously.

Auguste looked up and saw them coming. He left the mounted stranger and ran toward them, carrying a paper in his hand. They stopped the cart, waiting apprehensively for him. Julie kept staring at the stranger, trying to recognize what was familiar about him.

"Philippe!" Her surprised cry startled the other two.

"It is! What's de Vauve doing here?" asked Didier.

"Oh," is all Jeanne said.

Auguste stopped in front of Julie. "I don't know what to make of this," he said, waving the paper. "I know Monsieur Jacques promised us a leader whose name he couldn't reveal, but I can't believe it could be him!"

Julie's mouth dropped open. "But you are our leader," she said, staring at Auguste.

He looked down at the ground. "No, I didn't have the freedom to move about and make arrangements. I was to lead if anything happened to our appointed leader." Julie kept staring in disbelief.

Didier said, "This don't seem right. Maybe that paper is forged."

Auguste handed the paper to Julie. "Ju...Joel should be able to tell," he said.

Julie read the blind man's scraggly letter aloud:

"Dear Children,
    You are truly my spiritual children, though not my natural ones. Therefore, your safety and welfare are my only concerns. For this reason, I have prevailed upon Philippe de Vauve to conduct you safely to your destination. You must realize that his experience and knowledge of travel and affairs of government will be invaluable to you. For your safety, I could not reveal this information sooner. Follow him faithfully, trust him implicitly. Give him the obedience and support you would give me.

God be with you,
Jacques."

"He's not even a Huguenot!" Didier exploded.
"What do you think, Joel?" Auguste asked.
"Why ask him? We know Monsieur Jacques better'n him," protested Didier.
Julie rubbed the back of her neck and pursed her lips, wanting to believe in Philippe but knowing everyone's safety might rest on this decision. Philippe's embittered spirit conflicted with the love the Huguenots shared for one another. Yet, Jacques seemed to trust him.
"I do know," she said slowly, "that Jacques often received a night visitor whose face I was never allowed to see. Also, a stranger attended the service the last night, hidden in the lilac bushes. I believe Jacques arranged that. Could that stranger have been Philippe de Vauve?"
"There! I know he's all right," Jeanne said, her face glowing. "I think it's a brilliant plan. Who would suspect this gentleman of leading a band of Huguenots from the country. I trust him."
For some reason, this ruffled Julie's spirits. "Still, we can't be too

careful," she warned.

"We can't refuse him," Auguste said, "because if he's against us, our only hope is to let him think we trust him, and watch him closely as we travel. He would turn us back, for sure, if he's one of them and we refused to let him come with us."

"'Tis true," agreed Didier.

"You're all being ridiculous!" snorted Jeanne.

They prodded the mule and continued their approach to the mill. Philippe touched his hat in greeting, then rode off the road onto a cart path toward the forest.

"He knows our plans. He's heading straight to where the children are hiding," said Auguste, motioning to Didier to follow with the cart. Julie had expected them to be hiding in the mill but they came bounding out of a shepherd's cottage, which was out of sight from the main road. They gleefully greeted the older ones.

Philippe, who was avoiding and ignoring Julie, turned to Auguste, "Have I convinced you of my credentials, General?" His smile covered up the sarcasm from everyone but Julie and, possibly, Auguste.

"No, Captain, but I'm ready to follow you," he answered.

"Good. First, we'll substitute Chestnut for this tortoise you have hitched to the cart. We may not be able to keep the cart for the whole trip, depending on the roads. Some of them have been flooded by the rains."

"We need the cart, for the tapestries," Auguste reminded him.

"If we're forced to leave it, we must each lash a tapestry onto our back, since the tapestries are our security, our guarantee of funds." Philippe faced the younger children, saying, "You children must walk, except when absolutely too tired. Only then may you ride, for you must build up endurance as quickly as possible. We must be in La Rochelle in four days or we will miss our ship."

He addressed Auguste again. "If anything happens to some of us, the remainder must keep going. We're to contact a Captain Bailly, captain of the Dutch ship called 'The Floating Gull.'"

"What route do we follow?" asked Auguste.

"Mainly the back roads, which will be slower but safer. We might follow the highway after we pass Poitiers. I've arranged for fresh horses for the cart along the way, as well as for food and lodging."

"You've planned well for us, Monsieur de Vauve," Jeanne's admiring eyes were upon Philippe.

Philippe made a gracious bow in Jeanne's direction. "I was fortunate to have the freedom and the means to move about without coming under suspicion," he said.

Julie yearned to resume her natural role as a young woman. Now that they were safely out of Aubusson, there was no need for secrecy.

"I think it's time for everyone to know someth..." she began.

Philippe suddenly turned upon her, shouting, roughly, "Joel, why aren't you helping with that mule? Don't you know we've got to get started?"

"But, see here ..."

"You heard me, get busy!" he roared. She hurried to do his bidding, for Auguste had stiffened, his face beginning to flush with anger. She must not let Auguste and Philippe clash.

Julie released the mule. "I'll show you where to put him," spoke Philippe at her side. She followed him beyond the cottage, watching him tie the mule's reins securely to a tree.

"Why did you stop me from saying who I am? We're out of Aubusson and I'm sick of this disguise."

Philippe straightened. "I thought that's what you were about to announce, you little fool! Don't you realize that your very presence in this group increases the danger for everyone? As long as no one knows your identity, they are a bit safer. What if we're stopped and questioned?"

"You're just afraid I'd shirk my share of the work as a girl! That's it, isn't it? You like to see me working like a slave, humbling myself before you, having to lick your boots," she stormed.

"Humble? Hah!" retorted Philippe, just as hotly. Then he lowered his voice, "Auguste knows, doesn't he?"

"Yes."

"I knew it, that proves my point. His behavior toward you is entirely different from the others. We don't need any love-sick gallants on this trip!"

"Why, you despicable pig," Julie exclaimed. "You're not worthy to lead this group. Whatever was my father thinking?"

Philippe scowled down upon her. "Don't you even mention your father to me. After all your high-sounding declarations about your loyalty and love for him, here you are, running away from him again! You're a fraud. I've been right about you all the time." Turning on his heels, he stalked away before she could answer.

Julie stood, considering his words resentfully. Philippe, who knew nothing of Jacques' death, had no idea that she had rejected the plan of leaving Aubusson. Like him, she believed it would have been a second desertion of her father. She wondered, fleetingly, if Jacques had perhaps welcomed death, knowing that only then would she obey his wishes to leave with the others.

Auguste bounded down the path toward her, urgently calling, "Come on, we're leaving." He stopped when he saw her face. "What's wrong?"

"Philippe doesn't think I should reveal who I am."

"I agree with him on that. Your life is in desperate danger, and we have to get you safely away from here. Besides," he added, grinning, "you make a terrific-looking boy."

She hurried after him, and they fell in behind the cart with the others. Chestnut, after several puzzled glances behind him at the cart, pulled it at a quick pace. They soon left the main road to Limoges and turned north. At noon, they stopped for a brief rest and a cold lunch.

After unhitching Chestnut from the wagon, Philippe rode away. He returned promptly with a fresh horse. "Now I can use Chestnut for scouting," he announced, as he helped them hitch up the new horse to the cart.

When they stopped for lunch, Julie tumbled into the grass and fell almost instantly to sleep. She was still too tired to eat when Auguste tried to rouse her. Struggling to regain her senses, she vaguely heard the others conversing.

"I tell you, he's got to ride in the cart. He's been awake since early yesterday and is still soaking wet from last night. Do you want a sick traveler?" Auguste demanded.

"After all, if it weren't for Joel, the Boulard children, my brothers, Auguste – none of them would be here," said Jeanne.

"What do you mean?" Philippe asked. In spite of her efforts to stay awake, Julie dozed off again while the others described last night's adventures. She roused only briefly when some strong arms lifted her into the cart. She sank gratefully into the tapestries while steady hands gently covered her, completely hiding her. She slept deeply until the sun was sinking into the forest.

Wonderfully refreshed by her sleep, Julie jumped to the ground and marched with the others toward the sunset. It seemed symbolic of the western land they sought to embrace with their new lives, the land of their dreams, the land where they would find safety and freedom. She felt lighthearted and unfettered, in spite of the sorrows and dangers that hovered all around them. As she exchanged glances with Auguste, she knew he understood.

Chapter XVIII
Pursued

As they trudged down the road, Julie looked around for Philippe. The crowded road on which they traveled was clearly a major highway.

"Where are we, Auguste?" she asked.

"We're between L'Abbaye and La Croiserie. I don't like the looks of this road – too many travelers. Someone is sure to remember us."

"And Philippe?"

"Ah, so it's Philippe," he chided her. "Naturally, you call him by his surname. You're both born high above a simple man like me."

"Auguste, one thing I learned from Jacques: never judge a friend by his birth. Now, tell me where our distinguished leader is – scouting?"

"So he claims. I must admit, he has done nothing suspicious yet."

In the fields on Julie's right, a group of peasants were ending their long day's work. The men loaded two farm carts with produce while the women gathered the farm tools. Two men added a straw and dirt covering to the neat oblong mound where they had buried roots for winter storage.

Julie turned at the sound of a rushing horse. Philippe appeared suddenly in their midst. His tone and expression commanded immediate, unquestioning obedience.

"Quick, into the field over there," he shouted. "Take your places among the peasants and pretend you're one of them. You children, run fast to that pasture over there and begin playing a game, any game.

The rest of you act busy!"

They turned the cart into the field and stopped it near a tall haystack. Auguste frantically threw straw on top the cart. Philippe galloped across the field and talked with a tall farmer. Julie saw the flash of coins exchanging hands. The farmer nodded and hurriedly spoke to the peasants. Philippe unsaddled Chestnut and left him with the carthorses tethered nearby.

Didier helped a peasant hand out farm tools to the older boys while the younger ones scurried toward the pasture. After leaving his horse, Philippe rushed back across the field, stumbling often as he sank ankle deep in the soft, wet earth.

When he reached Julie, he grabbed her by the arm and seized Jeanne's arm with his other hand. In his haste, he half dragged them to the haystack and motioned them to the ground. He shoved Julie's head onto Jeanne's lap.

"Now, act like lovers! Your lives might depend upon your performance." He rubbed mud onto his clothes and face. He was busy at work with a rake in his hands by the time a detachment of soldiers rode into sight.

Through half-closed eyes, Julie recognized the dashing figure of the marquis in the lead. She caught her breath, looked up into Jeanne's face, and saw that her eyes were closed and her lips were moving. It was indeed a good time to pray, Julie decided.

Jeanne leaned over Julie and gently stroked her brow. "Don't take this seriously, you goat," she whispered, her blue eyes twinkling, in spite of her fear.

"Oh, I'm not that bad, am I?" Julie carried the farce on, realizing that cuddling the apprentice wasn't what Jeanne desired. "I'll wager you wish Philippe were in my place." Jeanne blushed.

The soldiers stopped in the road. Philippe and Auguste worked several yards from the highway, ignoring the soldiers.

"Halloo!" shouted one soldier who approached the haystack on horseback. Jeanne looked up as the soldier doffed his hat and smiled, "Tell me, fair Demoiselle, if you've seen a group of young children traveling this way in the company of an old blind man?"

"No, sir." Jeanne did not stop stroking Julie's brow.

"The man might be hidden in a wagon," the soldier persisted. "We've traced some young travelers but no one has seen a blind man."

"I can't help you, sir. I only just finished my work. I got no time to watch the world pass by," said Jeanne.

"Ah, yes, so I see," as the soldier gave a significant glance at the boy reclining on her lap. He turned to face the marquis, who had ridden up to them.

The marquis guided his splendid horse to within inches of Jeanne and Julie before stopping. He looked down at them. Julie hoped that her quaking didn't show and felt Jeanne's hand trembling on her brow.

"Tell me, would your lazy friend like to earn a few pennies? I need a lad who knows this country. We think our fugitives are traveling on the back roads. Know you the country, lad? Get up when addressed by your superior," the marquis snapped.

From the corner of her eyes, still half closed, Julie saw that Auguste and Philippe had both frozen in place. Jeanne stiffened and the Lafaud boys stopped working to watch with dread.

Julie started to stand up, fell back, then rose slowly with apparent difficulty to her feet. She looked toward the marquis, but avoided meeting his eyes. She twisted her mouth and stuttered, "I ... I'm honored b...by your Honor's w...wishes, sir. I...I'll go with you, g...gladly." All this Julie said in a pained, stupid manner while the marquis stared down at her. He looked not at her face, but at her right foot, upon which she put no weight. She dragged her foot stiffly, as though crippled. As she made a jump or two upon her "good" leg toward him, the marquis wheeled his horse around.

"Never mind, you're no use to me," he called back as he rode away to rejoin his band.

"Joel, you were magnificent," whispered Jeanne, as Julie sank back to the ground. They watched the soldiers ride off down the highway. Only Auguste and Philippe could fathom the danger and fright she had just experienced, face to face with the madman who sought her life. For the first time that day, she was glad she had listened to Philippe and kept her identity hidden.

"Why would he think that Jacques was with us?" demanded Philippe, as he strode up with a puzzled frown. When Auguste started to speak Julie hushed him. Philippe looked from one to the other.

"Go call the children and get them ready," Philippe said to Jeanne, and she rushed to obey.

"Now," he continued, "What's the big secret between you two." Auguste looked away from Philippe toward Julie, refusing to speak unless she so directed. Any answer from him was unnecessary. Julie's trembling lips and tear-filled eyes gave her away. Philippe's spirit crumbled before her eyes, and his body stiffened, motionless. His eyes begged for a denial.

Julie spoke softly. "He died yesterday morning at dawn, quietly and peacefully. Lucienne and I buried him in the grove. The others don't know." She turned and walked away.

With long strides, Phillipe easily overtook her. Choking back tears, he struggled to speak. "Forgive me, Julie. I didn't know when I scolded you this morning."

Julie was silent. Philippe spoke again. "But I wish you would explain this." He pulled out from under his shirt the missing Bible that Jacques had given her the day before. With a cry of delight, she seized it.

"Oh, his Bible! He gave it to me ... I promised to keep it and use it, but I lost it." Her voice was a whisper as she remembered, aloud, "I was reading it to him when he died."

Philippe's face softened. "I'm so relieved, Julie. I thought you stole it from him and threw it away."

Julie looked at him, horrified. "You really think I'm despicable, don't you. You never think anything but the worst of me." She ran ahead to rejoin the others.

Phillipe watched her rush away. He kicked a rock and then trudged toward Chestnut with heavy steps. Then Phillipe suddenly stopped, straightened his shoulders, and quickly saddled Chestnut. He led Chestnut briskly to the others, who huddled together awaiting instructions. "Let's go before these curious folk start asking questions."

They followed the highway only a short distance. Then Philippe led them onto a road that was little more than a path, leading into a thick forest. Darkness descended suddenly as the trees blotted out the evening sky. The children no longer straggled, but kept as near as possible to the cart.

Philippe stopped in front of a small chapel used by hunters. It needed repairs, but would make ideal overnight quarters for this group. Philippe led the cart out of sight behind the building.

"Now for a bite to eat," said Philippe, gathering little Matt Boulard into his arms. "You've been great little soldiers today," he said, looking at all the children. The Boulard twins pressed close to Julie, whom they regarded as a hero since last night's dramatic rescue.

Jeanne distributed bread, salted meat, and cheese. They were all famished but the children were so tired they could hardly finish the meal.

"The children and girls will sleep in the chapel. Didier, Auguste, and I will stay with the cart."

Jeanne objected, "I'm willing to do 'most anything, but I won't sleep in an idol-worshipper's church."

"It will keep the dew off." Philippe looked surprised. "Besides, I don't see that you have any choice."

"But I'm a Huguenot!" she exclaimed.

"Aw, do what he says, unless you want to sleep in the woods with the wolves," said her brother.

Julie saw Philippe smile into Jeanne's eyes. "I thought you folks could find God anywhere," he said softly. "Don't tell me He won't take care of you in a Catholic chapel."

Jeanne started to speak, then smiled. "All right, I'll stay there."

"What about Joel?" Auguste looked quizzically at Philippe while Julie hid a smile. Philippe had left Julie out of the instructions, forgetting she could sleep neither with the "girls and children" nor with the men. Evening confusion over Joel's bedtime arrangements seemed to be a recurring problem for Philippe de Vauve. He had planned everything about this trip so beautifully and carefully, Julie was delightedly amused by his present predicament.

Didier snorted, "What's wrong with the cart – there's enough room."

Auguste and Philippe exchanged embarrassed glances, then looked quickly away. Finally, Julie rescued the two young men.

"Someone should sleep in the porch of the church to make sure nothing startles the girls and children. I'll sleep in the doorway."

Though Julie slept on a folded tapestry, her bed was hard and cold. A nightingale serenaded its mate from the deep forest. An owl hooted uncomfortably near her pallet. After a distant wolf howled, she was happy that the men brought the cart to the front of the chapel and parked it close to the porch. Then she relaxed into a deep sleep, not stirring until a chorus of birds coaxed her awake the next morning.

Chapter XIX
La Rochelle

Three days later Philippe stopped the travelers on top of a small hill. "There lies La Rochelle," he announced, waving his right arm toward the city that clustered around a busy seaport. The sun was sinking into a scarlet and orange ocean, making purple silhouettes of the toy-like ships anchored there. Ghostly ruins of the La Rochelle fort overlooked the bay. Booming church bells from the city announced Sunday evening vespers.

"We have you to thank for our safe arrival," said Jeanne, as she moved to his side. "You have led us through one danger after another. God sent you to lead us."

"It was the cooperation of everyone," Philippe replied.

"Jeanne is right, de Vauve. We couldn't have made the trip without you. God chose you, for sure," added Auguste. Philippe's hand fell on Auguste's thick shoulder. Julie saw the two young men smile warmly at each other.

"You would have done the same job without me," Philippe assured Auguste.

As usual, as soon as Philippe stopped the cart, the tired children sprawled along the roadside to steal a few moments rest. As Julie looked at them, her heart swelled with love and pride. How bravely they had traveled, with hardly any complaining. The Boulard boys, like the others, regarded Philippe with worshipful eyes.

He turned and smiled at the children. "We're here. Our journey is over. Now you'll have a sea voyage in one of those big ships out there," as he pointed to the horizon. Then he turned back to face Auguste. "It will be risky to enter town with this cart of stolen tapestries, especially since they were stolen from the king," he laughed. "But we'll try. I wish I had my uniform. I could bluff our way through the gate."

The ruins of a smaller fort were scattered on top of a slight rise on the left side of the road. This fort, as well as the large one in the harbor, had been destroyed during the fierce battles of La Rochelle. Here the kings of France had crushed the military might of the Huguenots, long ago.

Philippe and Auguste guided the group toward the ruins. "We'll be hidden from the road here," said Philippe. "Unfortunately, we're late. This was our day to board ship."

Auguste protested, "We thought it was tomorrow."

"In this one thing Jacques was mistaken. Last week I contacted representatives of Captain Bailly, so we're expected. I asked them to wait for us one day, in case we were delayed. But we must not be delayed. The captain hopes to sail tonight."

They reached the grassy interior of the ruins where the crumbling walls hid the city and road from view. The children tumbled into tired heaps, some of them falling instantly to sleep.

"I must go ahead and see how conditions are in the city. Auguste, you stay here. If I don't come back before midnight, you take over." Philippe mounted Chestnut and rode away.

Jeanne, Auguste, and Julie watched the rider descend toward the road. When he paused and looked back, they waved encouragingly. Julie had a lump in her throat. Philippe had to come back safely.

She sat down upon a stone near the children and drew Jacques' Bible from a pouch that she now wore hidden under her shirt. She felt guilty she hadn't read it since her escape began, yet, there had been time for nothing but urgent flight and exhausted sleep.

To her surprise, when she opened the Bible the pages parted to reveal an envelope addressed to Julie Mirovar. When she opened the envelope, age-browned papers fell into her lap.

"How curious," she called to Auguste and Jeanne. "These are Jacques' identity papers, his credentials as a Huguenot minister. I thought he was only a lay preacher."

"We didn't know he was a minister, either, until our pastor died and no one came to take his place. Then Monsieur Jacques told us he was an ordained pastor, and he became our leader. But he never gave up his weaving." said Jeanne.

"He combined weaving with the work of the church. The officials granted him more freedom and importance as a weaver than they ever would have to a Huguenot pastor."

Julie wondered why Jacques wanted her to have these papers. After examining them carefully, she returned the papers to the Bible but she tore the envelope with her name on it into tiny pieces. When it became too dark to read, she curled up like the children and slept under the clear, starlit sky.

Philippe's arrival awakened her, still early in the evening. She, with Jeanne and Auguste, listened eagerly to his report. "There's quite an upheaval in town. The streets are swarming with soldiers, but they seem purposeless. Something big is underway. Rumors say that the king has signed a revocation of the Edict of Nantes."

Auguste paced, agitated. "Monsieur Jacques was afraid this was about to happen, but he hoped we'd be safely away first."

Jeanne looked at the three distressed faces of her companions. "What are you talking about?" she demanded.

Julie hurried to explain, secretly glad she knew more than Jeanne did about such an important matter. "It means the king has revoked the only law that offered any protection to non-Catholics. It means that all Protestant churches will be destroyed and all Huguenots are outlaws, subject to death or imprisonment!" When Julie saw the look on Jeanne's face, she regretted her words. She remembered that this sentence would fall on Jeanne's family, indeed, on all the families left behind in Aubusson.

"It also means escape from France will be even more difficult, for it is now forbidden. We will make it, though," Philippe stated, grimly. "Guards block every entrance to and exit from the waterfront, but guards can be bought. It will take a great sum to escape France, but that is why Jacques gave us these tapestries."

"Won't it be dangerous to try to sell the king's tapestries?" asked Auguste.

"This is a good town in which to try it. La Rochelle has many rich citizens who have no love for the king. Such beautiful tapestries, impossible to buy legally, should command excellent prices."

"How do we find these citizens without getting arrested?" Auguste asked.

"I know a Count de Cholet here who should be interested in our merchandise. I'll write a letter of introduction for you, Auguste. We have often discussed Aubusson tapestries, and he has complained that the king has refused to sell him any."

By the light of an improvised torch, Philippe wrote the letter. He handed Chestnut's reins to Auguste, saying, "I think it's safer for you to go on this mission. You should have no trouble finding the house. On Chestnut you should make good time."

Auguste returned shortly with good news. "After your letter finally reached the count, he was very good to me. He scolded the servant who thought my business was too trivial for his master. He told me to return immediately with the tapestries."

"Splendid! Perhaps he'll buy Chestnut, too," said Philippe.

They woke up the sleepy children, promising them that their hard journey was almost over. They seemed subdued and spent as they followed the cart back onto the highway. Julie noticed that Zachary rode in the cart again, as he had for most of the day.

When the cart reached the city gate, Philippe was already there talking to the guards. Julie was sure their smooth entry through the gate cost him a handsome bribe.

"Head for the cathedral square," he called back to them, as he rode ahead on Chestnut. When they caught up with him behind the cathedral, he was stroking his horse, talking to him in a low voice. Then, turning away and striding to the cart, he threw back the dusty canvas that covered the weavings. After groping under the surface, he found what he was looking for.

"Here, Auguste, help me tie this on my back. We will sell all the tapestries except this one. You and the older boys, with Chestnut, will take as many tapestries as you can carry to the count. If he wants more, come back for the remainder. See if the count will buy the horse. I will stay with Jeanne and the children. Joel must stay, too."

"Why can't Joel help carry these heavy tapestries?" demanded Didier.

Auguste restrained him, saying, "Obviously, Philippe and Joel have good reasons for not seeing Count de Cholet." Like the others, Julie had become so accustomed to obeying Philippe that she didn't argue, even though she wanted to go with Auguste to see the transaction.

Phillipe chose to wait with the cart in a small market square. The Sunday merchants had long since taken their produce and returned home. The five elm trees in the center of the square sheltered the waiting group. Julie was leaning against the almost empty cart when Thomas sidled up to her. "Joel," he whispered, "come look at Zachary. I think he's real sick."

She walked up to Zachary, his head propped against a tree. She drew in her breath as she felt the twin's forehead. "You're right, Thomas, he has fever. How long has he been like this?"

"Since yesterday. I've been helping him. He didn't want to delay us, so he wouldn't let me tell anybody. Jeanne would get all excited and make too much fuss, so I came to you."

Julie looked from one twin to the other, and realized why all the children had been favoring Zachary, why they insisted he take extra turns riding in the cart, why they helped him when they stopped, why they furnished him with extra portions of drinking water.

"You're brave, wonderful soldiers, and I'm very proud of you," she whispered. "Do you think you can hold out until we reach the ship? It might be very soon, now."

Zachary lifted his head, his little chin set with determination. "I can. I'm fine. I just need to rest a little."

Julie sat down by Zachary, who gladly let her pull his head into her lap. Thomas cuddled up to her on the other side. Relief flooded his features, as he released his heavy burden of anxiety to Julie.

"Monsieur Jacques used to come pray when one of us got sick. S'pose you could do that?" he asked her, timidly.

"I'm not sure I know how," she said.

"Oh, it's easy. You see, God is right here next to us, so you talk to Him like you could see Him, like you and me are talking right now."

Julie remembered how a desperate prayer for help at the monastery had given her courage. "I'll try," she said.

After an awkward moment, she faltered, "Lord, we're very young and tired and now one of our little soldiers is sick. We are powerless to outwit all these enemies by ourselves so ... take over, God. And, especially help Zachary to be all right." Julie sat still a moment, trying to sense if God was really there. "Thank you for listening," she whispered.

"Amen," Thomas' small voice chimed. "You forgot that, Joel."

Julie and the two children sat in comfortable silence, Zachary dozing with his head in her lap, Thomas' hand in hers. She could overhear Philippe and Jeanne talking.

"Will you leave us when we board ship, Monsieur de Vauve, or do you leave France, too?"

Philippe laughed softly. "Surely, Jeanne, after these days on the road with me, you can call me Philippe. I'm going to the Netherlands, also."

"Why are you leaving, Philippe?" Her voice was soft. "You aren't one of us."

"I'm not sure, Jeanne. I have more searching and thinking to do before I know the answer. I admire your faith, but I can not believe that only the Huguenots, or only the Catholics, hold the door to God. Why should God make himself available to only one church?"

"Why, because we have the Word, so we follow the true faith."

"If the Bible is the key, why can't it help a man find God? Why do Huguenots, like their enemies, insist that I must come into their church and theirs alone if I want to find God?"

"I don't know about other churches, Philippe. I do know that God is very real to me in mine."

"I believe you. But for me, both churches in France are too militant, demanding that members make war on others in order to convert them by force. This I cannot accept."

"I'm sorry you have no faith." There was a catch in Jeanne's voice.

"Please don't cry, Jeanne. I'm touched by your concern. Does your Book not say that when men seek God they will find Him? I assure you, dear Jeanne, I'm seeking with all my heart."

"Then you will become one of us!" Jeanne answered, confidently. "Will you stay in Holland?"

"No, I hope to go on to the New World. I've heard that in some of the colonies men are free to worship God and make a living however they please. I think I belong where no one church can dictate to all people."

"What will you do for a living?"

"I don't know, but I hear it's a country where a young man can build a good future."

"I hear there are very few women over there," Jeanne's voice was so low that Julie had to strain to hear it.

Julie felt strangely disturbed by the sight of Jeanne and Philippe silhouetted against the starlit sky. They reminded her of the tapestry now hanging at Valjean. She remembered Philippe's words to her when they were children: "Someday I shall find the girl in that tapestry – a sweet, gentle, feminine girl. I shall never marry until I find her."

Even then, Julie knew he was teasing her for preferring to romp and roam, to ride and climb, for lacking interest in the gentle arts of womanhood. She thought how well Jeanne measured up to these ideals, while she still played the part of a boy, though circumstances now forced this role upon her.

She sat motionless, awaiting Philippe's response. After a moment it came, clear and determined. "I know, that is why I plan to take my woman with me."

The older boys tumbled back into the square, saying, "Give us all the other tapestries. The count wants all we have." As they staggered off with tapestries on backs and shoulders, Auguste stopped in front of Philippe, who still had a tapestry strapped across his back. "Are you sure you don't want to sell that one, too?" he asked.

"It's not mine to sell, Auguste. It stays with me."

"As you say," Auguste said as he marched off to catch up with the others.

When the boys returned, Auguste plopped a bag into Philippe's hands. "There you are. The count was satisfied and I think you will be with the sum. Something strange happened as we were leaving."

"What do you mean?" asked Philippe, suddenly alert.

"No one was in the hall but the count and us. He said, 'Port number fourteen is the safest and cheapest, and I wish you bon voyage.' I was so surprised I didn't answer, and he repeated the same message twice more. Do you suppose he knows our mission?"

"I'm sure he guesses it, and I trust him. We'll try his suggestion. Let's go."

Philippe divided them into three small groups to avoid attracting unwanted attention. Philippe led with the Matin and Bigot children, Auguste and Julie followed with the doctor's three boys, and Jeanne and her four brothers came last. They left the cart in the square.

The children's eyes opened wide as they saw the brightly uniformed soldiers, the fancy coaches, and the festive cafes. Julie stayed near Zachary, watching him carefully, whispering encouragement to him as they plodded toward the sea.

The smell of the harbor assured Julie they must be near the port. Of one accord, they all increased their pace. Suddenly the harbor spread out before them. Philippe paused only a moment, then went on as though he knew where he was going.

Soldiers with muskets patrolled the area. A guard stopped a family of three entering the harbor area. As Julie's group moved on, she heard desperate arguing, waving of papers, and earnest pleas, but she passed too quickly to see the outcome of this confrontation.

When Julie's group rounded a curve along the crowded waterfront, Philippe and his group had disappeared. The Lafauds caught up with Julie's group as they hesitated to look for their leader. Then Philippe appeared, alone.

"I've found a good hiding place for all of you down this alley. See? The ruins of an old boat. Wait here in absolute silence until I return. Didier will go with me, for two men are less likely to have trouble from robbers. Auguste, it's more important for you to stay here, in case we don't get back."

Julie wondered if Jeanne's involuntary cry was for Philippe or her brother. "Philippe hasn't failed to come back yet, has he," said Julie.

The suspense and forced silence made the time drag. A bright moon rose making them visible to one another. Philippe and Didier returned so silently, they were in their midst before anyone heard them.

"It's arranged. Let's go," said Philippe. He urged them on until they faced a big, burly guard who wielded an ugly musket and club.

"Now?" Philippe asked him. The guard gave a surly nod. When Philippe and the guard turned their backs, Didier whispered, "Quick, follow me."

They scrambled beyond the built-up bulwarks protecting the harbor and ducked into the shadow of a great pier. In bright moonlight, rows of beached fisher craft lined the shore before them.

A few larger craft anchored a short distance from shore. Julie saw three big ships out in the water. Was one of these their ship?

They huddled together until Philippe joined them. "We must stay out of sight of the guards above," he said. "I must find someone to ferry us to the Floating Gull."

"Do you still have money," worried Auguste.

"Oh, yes. The guard drove a hard bargain, but if he had known how much we have left for our passage, his price would have been much dearer."

Again, Philippe left them while they waited beneath the pier in silence. Julie watched him stride down the beach to a group of fishermen straightening their nets. He stepped away from the group with a short, sturdy man with stooped shoulders and gestured toward the open sea. They argued. When Phillipe started back toward the pier, the fisherman walked beside him.

"This is Monsieur Gond," Philippe introduced him. "He says it's very dangerous to attempt a ferry job tonight because of the bright moonlight. He says the seas are patrolled, as well as the shore.

However, he has agreed to load us into his boat, hide it beneath the pier, and wait for a cloudy sky. If clouds come, he will take us to the ship, and we will pay him double. If not, we will pay him the agreed price, even if we are still here at dawn. His job is complete at dawn, regardless. Do you accept this agreement?"

Julie squinted at the sky, which appeared hopelessly clear and cloudless. How discouraging to be so near freedom and be stopped by the moon. Everyone else agreed gladly to the strange bargain. Monsieur Gond left to fetch his boat.

"There's not a cloud in sight," Julie protested. "Why are you so confident this will work?"

Jeanne reached over and gave her hand a squeeze. "Have faith, Joel. God wouldn't bring us this far if He didn't plan for us to succeed."

Monsieur Gond glided his boat silently among the crowded fishing boats. The water was too shallow to bring the boat under the pier. "Can't load up, then," said the fisherman. "Got to wait there." He climbed out of the boat, secured it, and joined them under the pier.

Julie and Philippe anxiously scanned the sky from time to time, but the others waited with confidence. Julie marveled at their trust.

"Sure glad to see some strong arms amongst ye," announced the old fisherman. "A fella needs help rowin' a boat load like this – if we git away," he added.

Julie tried to stretch her cramped legs without disturbing Zachary. The feverish child found comfort in snuggling up to her. It was well past midnight, and the children were asleep, again.

"Shhhh," whispered the fisherman, needlessly. On the pier above them, footsteps paused.

"Well, shouldn't have trouble tonight," a man's voice said.

"No sir, bright moon like that puts the favors on our side," came a second voice.

"You sure nobody's come past you tonight, huh?"

"I'm sure, sir. Can't see why this job is so important, though. Nobody but poor refugees ever tries to get by. They can't swim to the North Countries."

"Don't underestimate those people. You kill one and ten more will spring up to take his place. Back them up against a sea or a wall of mountains and they'll disappear before your eyes. It's a stinking business but it's our job."

"Yes, sir."

"Besides, we're now working under direct orders of the king. He doesn't want France to lose any more citizens so he has forbidden all Huguenots to emigrate." The footsteps faded.

Julie felt no desire to sleep. She searched the skies for clouds until her eyes ached. She gazed longingly once more toward where the big ships lay at anchor, but she couldn't see them. She decided she must be sleepier than she thought. Then she stiffened with excitement: she couldn't see the big ships because fog had rolled in. There was hope after all.

Chapter XX
The Floating Gull

"How is Zachary?" Philippe asked Julie as he moved across the sand to crouch beside her. He had noticed Zachary's weakness, and Julie had told him that the child had a high fever.

Julie was still staring toward the hidden ships. "Look," she exclaimed, not hearing his question. Philippe followed her gaze, then shook the dozing fisherman's shoulder.

"Wake up, man, and see what's happening!"

The old fisherman sat up quickly. "Well, what ye know," he said, rubbing his eyes. "He done it again."

"What did you say?" whispered Julie.

"He done it again. If ye be true Huguenot, ye know what I mean." Julie shook her head, bewildered.

The moonlight shone on the man's face as he spoke. "Looky here, I been fishin' out o' this harbor all my life. I been seein' folks like these goin' off with hope in their faces right under the nose of them powerful soldiers, always watchin' up there. Maybe a little bit of them Huguenots rubbed off on me, 'cause I got to admit, this is more fun than bringin' in fish."

"You mean, you think God is deliberately sending fog so this handful of people can ride your boat?" Philippe sounded doubtful.

"No, no, I didn't say that, not 'zactly," he hedged. "But if I was a Huguenot, I might be sayin' it."

The swirling fog became thicker, slowly but steadily. The fishing boats melted into shadowy hulks; the moon dissolved into the mist. Julie was awed by the mysterious drama which was unfolding. She believed the fisherman was right about the fog, only, why should God bother to intercede for a group of insignificant emigrants? He must love His children very much, she thought.

And He must love her. Images from the past week flashed across her mind. She knew she was smart, but surely it had taken more than cleverness to get her out of all those scrapes. Maybe God was there – to provide her with escape clothes, to hide her identity from Albert's servant, to help her past the guards at the Valjean castle, to hand her peasant clothes and food at the Vagran hut, to convince Phillipe against his judgment to take her on as servant, to defeat the bandits single-handed, to rescue the children, … and to arrive just in time for the escape and just in time to spend his last days with her father. And her father, despite blindness, harassment, soldiers, and illness, seemed so full of inner joy and peace.

She felt unusually alive and vibrant, as God the Shepherd became very real to her. "Oh please, Lord. Be my Shepherd, too!" she whispered, earnestly.

Her heart caught when Philippe leaned against her and whispered, "Are you all right?"

"I was never more at peace, Philippe," she confided as a strange new awareness swept through her. Like her father and Lucienne, she would never be alone again. She could always talk to God.

Julie had found faith!

Monsieur Gond moved toward his boat. The children were wakened. The fisherman gave instructions in a loud whisper.

"Take it easy. Sit there, no, here. Move over closer. Let the big 'un sit there. Careful, the boat is too loaded. Ach," he cried out, as the boat dragged on the rocky bottom.

Philippe started to climb aboard when the boat dragged. He

pushed, but the boat was stuck. Julie had entered the boat last, and before anyone realized what she was doing, she jumped out and stood beside Philippe. Immediately, the boat lifted, floating free.

The fisherman's hoarse whisper now revealed panic. "Hey, now, we can't make it if we take on two more. I thought with the children …"

Everyone in the boat sat in stunned silence. Philippe and Julie stood knee-deep in the water. Auguste started up, then sat again quickly as the boat wobbled dangerously. "Let me get out!"

"No, no … I need ye to row!"

"He's right, Auguste," said Philippe, looking desperately from the boat to Julie. "Monsieur, can't you just take this lad? He's so small he should make little difference," he pleaded as he shoved Julie toward the boat.

"No, I oughta make a couple o' children stay – the boat's overloaded. Sorry, but ye must act fast if ye want to make any changes. We got to move outa here."

"No exchanges!" Julie insisted.

"We must!" Auguste exclaimed.

"Listen to me," Julie pleaded. "Auguste is needed and all the children must go. The Lafaud family must not be separated, nor the others. Can't we find another boat?"

"Go see me brother, Andre Gond," urged the fisherman. "His shack's on the waterfront, so ye won't have to pass the guards. Ye may keep the other half of the pay to buy thy passage. Good luck!"

As the boatman shoved off with his oar, several faint cries arose. "Don't worry, we'll join you on ship. Ask Captain Bailly to hold off for as long as possible and, Jeanne," Philippe called, his voice low.

"Yes?" Her voice floated back to them.

"Jeanne, pray, keep on praying, all of you."

Philippe and Julie crept back to the edge of the pier. She clutched

Jacques' Bible as they watched the fishing boat disappear into the fog. She felt no fear as the boat moved out of sight and hearing, taking everyone except the two of them to safety and freedom.

Philippe stood up beside the pier and looked around, cautiously. "Well, Julie, it's the world against just you and me, again."

"No, Philippe," she whispered, emphatically, "there are three of us this time."

Philippe understood immediately, for he asked, "Is the daughter of Jacques now a Huguenot?"

The noise of running feet shut off her answer. Philippe grabbed her shoulders and heaved her under the pier so suddenly, she dropped the Bible in the sand. He swooped it up and ran off into the darkness.

"There goes one. I knew I heard voices." a deep voice bellowed overhead, on the pier.

"Stop, or I'll shoot you," shouted another. Julie burrowed into the sand until she had conccaled herself in the farthest dark corner beneath the pier. Philippe had offered himself as a decoy to protect her.

She heard him call, "Don't shoot, I'm not armed."

"How did you git down here? What are you up to? What's that in your hand?" There was no pause between questions.

"Can't a body come down to enjoy the ocean and meditate, without being treated like a criminal?" came Philippe's voice, in soothing tones.

"Look, he's got the Book in his hand. He's another one of them stubborn heretics."

"I heard voices. Let's look around." There was a thud in the sand when somebody jumped off the pier.

"You heard only myself," Philippe said. "I was talking out loud."

"Yeah, they do talk out loud to their God."

Julie could see shadows on the pier's underside, above her, as a torchlight was waved in search. She hardly breathed as she lay half-buried in the sand.

"Nothing under here. Maybe the crazy heretic is right."

Footsteps and voices receded into the distance, as did Philippe. As Julie scrambled from her hiding place in the sand, her hand fell upon a hard object whose jingle startled her. "The money bag. Philippe must have tossed it here."

She had two choices: she could remain on the beach and hire Andre Gond to take her to the Floating Gull, or she could follow Philippe. Though she knew she had little chance of helping him, she concealed the money in her smock and hurried toward the barricade. In the confusion, no one saw her slim figure dart through the shadows into the nearest alley. She had no difficulty following the noisy guard who had custody of Philippe.

Leaving the harbor behind, Philippe and his captor reached a big open square. Julie flattened herself on the ground behind a water trough as Philippe's captor escorted him to the campfire around which several soldiers sat. The city was so crowded, this group had to bivouac in the square. She placed herself where she could overhear their conversation.

"Look what my detachment found – add one more bounty to my account," the guard boasted.

"I advise you to wait 'til daylight to have him locked up. The jailer threatened to jail me, too, when I woke him awhile ago, taking in a couple I found," a reclining figure advised.

"All right, you. Sit down here, and don't try anything. They pay for dead heretics, too." The soldier squatted near the fire. Philippe stretched himself, yawned long and loudly, then lay down, and fell asleep.

"Ain't worried, is he?" queried an onlooker.

"Them's the kind that's hardest to handle. I'm keeping an eye on that one," declared the captor.

Julie wouldn't have believed she could sleep under such circumstances. But when she opened her eyes, the morning sun caused the gray fog to glow. Her eyes slowly focused, and suddenly a curious boy appeared above her. His body was tall and lanky, but he had a chubby, innocent face, and his golden hair shone in the morning light. He had come to water his master's horse at the public trough. Julie, still half-asleep, gaped at the drooling face of the horse directly above her own. The rippling laughter of the boy startled her.

"City's kind of crowded, ain't it," grinned the boy. "But I think I could have found you a better bed than that."

Julie glanced worriedly toward the group of soldiers in the square and saw Philippe still sprawled in sleep. She dusted the dirt from her clothes. "For a minute, there, I thought your horse was about to eat me," she grinned back.

"You look like you've been traveling," said the friendly boy as his eyes roved over her worn footwear and mud-caked clothing. "Where are your folks?"

"I ... I ... yes," she flushed. "I came with people from my village, but I lost them."

"I wager I know what happened. You were so busy gawking at city life, you let them walk off and leave you," he laughed.

"The city wakes up early," she observed, as a loud commotion approached along the street.

"Too early for me," the boy agreed, stifling a yawn.

They both turned to watch a group of five men. Iron chains clanked while two uniformed guards cursed the three captives they brought toward the square.

"It's him again, the Big One," said the boy. "Those are galley slaves. Every morning they hitch them to that post in the square for everybody to stare at as a warning to Huguenots who are thinking of leaving France. You see, they make galley slaves out of the ones they catch."

Julie shivered. She looked at Philippe, who was sitting up, rubbing the sleep from his eyes. She despised the thought of that life for her friend.

"These slaves are fresh from the galleys," the boy said.

A strange fascination drew her eyes back to the galley slaves who passed near her, especially the gaunt giant whose piercing dark eyes flashed with spirit. Her spine tingled as his eyes met hers. She was unable to tear her gaze from the powerful depths of fire reflected in those eyes. As he passed by, she gasped.

"Ain't he a terror? I think even the guards are scared of him. Galley slaves don't usually live long, but that one ...!" The boy paused to sit down on the edge of the trough. "That one has outlasted them all. You should hear the legends about the Big One."

So he's fascinated by him, too, Julie mused. She cringed as the burly guard who stood no higher than the Big One's arm pits drew back and hit the chained slave with his whip. The blood trickled from the cut and ran down the old scars that covered his bare chest. The Big One did not flinch. He held his chin high and set his mouth in a firm line. His indomitable eyes still flashed.

"Want something to eat?" the boy asked.

Julie was hungry, but she didn't want to leave the square. "No thanks, this is a good place to look for my companions."

The boy took a dark wheat cake from a saddlebag and broke it. He offered it to her, along with a piece of dried fish.

"Thanks, I wish I could repay you," she murmured.

"For this stale bread and smelly fish, hah," he snorted. Her thanks seemed to embarrass him.

The guards finished securing the galley slaves to a heavy piling in the square. As they walked toward the water trough, Philippe's captor hurried from the fireside to intercept the man who held the whip. They stopped a few feet from Julie and the boy. The guard gestured toward Philippe, now guarded by another soldier.

"Where did you find him?" asked the man with the whip.

"At the waterfront, last night, sir."

"Do you know who he is?"

"Yes, while he was sleeping I found his papers in his book." The guard said, proudly. "See, Jacques de Mirovar."

"Mirovar ... Mirovar," the man stood, pondering. "I know I've heard that name recently. You might have made a real catch, Corporal. Wait here until I can check my hunch."

Philippe had been watching the men discussing him. As they parted, his eyes met Julie's. He scowled, pursed his lips, and shook his head. He was trying every way, short of speech, to signal her to get away.

"Say, you know that man, don't you – that prisoner, I mean." The boy's words startled her. It was useless to deny it since he had seen Philippe's signals. He stared at her with new interest. "Is that the people you got lost from?" She nodded.

"That's rough, real rough." He was silent.

A few minutes later, a horse clattered toward them from out of the fog. The scarlet uniform of a special officer flashed by. The two guards, who had escorted the slaves, ran over to watch the officer dismount near the circle of soldiers. Julie's heart sank as she recognized the marquis. He must have guessed she would come to this port city to escape his power.

The marquis flung himself from one soldier to another like a madman, shouting, "Where is he? Where is this Jacques Mirovar? Show him to me!"

Julie, who averted her face from the marquis, was struck by the astounded expression on the Big One's face. He was as still as a bronze statue. He stared with overwhelming absorption at the marquis. His lips began to move, ever so slightly.

She glanced at Philippe, who turned white when he recognized the marquis. The guard who had escorted him pointed to Philippe.

"That – Jacques Mirovar? What are you guards trying to pull? Mirovar is an old man, stone-blind!" A crowd gathered to watch the ranting marquis. He swaggered over to Philippe.

"You! Could it be?" he sputtered. He grabbed Philippe by the collar, inspected him closely, and then released him. The wild look began to fade. He threw out his hands.

"I thought for a minute he could be her, disguised to pass for her father," he stammered. As these words passed his lips, the marquis stopped still. His face became clouded. "It is possible. She could pose as a man. That boy ... that boy in the field! No wonder his face has haunted me!" The marquis shouted again.

Julie knew her disguise was no longer safe. The marquis would now search for a boy. She shifted her position so that the curious crowd hid the marquis and Philippe from view. She could see the Big One clearly. He listened intensely, engrossed, to the marquis' words.

"What is your name, your real name?" the marquis demanded.

"I have never said it was Jacques de Mirovar," Philippe replied. "The soldiers said that."

"I'm asking you your name."

"I am Philippe de Pionsard de Vauve."

"You lie! What is the name of your brother?"

"Gerald de Pionsard de Vauve, Count of Aubusson, member of the king's court."

"Is it possible – but, of course it is! You would be from Aubusson, involved in the escape of a group of young persons, one in particular."

Philippe was silent while the marquis examined him with narrowed eyes. "Tell me, where is Mademoiselle de Beaulac?"

"I know no one of that name."

"You lie! Ah, I know. You know a Mademoiselle de Mirovar. "Where is she?"

He did not answer.

"I have the power to grant you your freedom if you will tell me what I wish to know. I will forgive your involvement, for no doubt she charmed you into helping her."

Still, he didn't answer.

"Answer me," the marquis screamed. Julie heard a loud whack and a gasp from the onlookers. She knew Philippe had been struck. She forgot herself and her own danger, and started moving toward Philippe.

Chapter XXI
Girl in the Tapestry

The boy grabbed Julie's arm. "Stop! Think!" Julie realized how foolish running up to Phillipe would be. Though she passionately yearned to block the blows falling on his back, she must avoid the angry marquis' frenzied eyes or all would be lost. Her mind was dazed and her body exhausted. Her eyes darted around the crowd, desperately hunting for any source of help, and again she felt mysteriously pulled to the big slave at the piling.

Big One's face hardened, and his eyes roved about the crowd, searching, jumping, finally settling on her as she knew they must. She began to inch toward him, amazed at his effect on her.

"I am your friend," the eyes beckoned. "Trust me!"

In a flash, Julie realized what to do and that it, however impossible, would work. She knew the Big One was unguarded and that the eyes of all were riveted on the marquis, except those of her new friend, who floated behind her, determined to protect her from further mishap.

"I'm going to set the Big One free," she whispered to him, pausing for his reaction.

The boy looked back at her in disbelief, but this time he quickly assented. His eyes grew bold with daring, and he grinned, "Let's!"

He whipped out a short sword and began sawing on the heavy ropes which bound the Big One's hands to the piling. Julie used her hunting knife to speed the job, wondering how to free the man's shackled feet. Even as she wondered, his hands fell free and, in one lightening movement, he grasped a large stone and shattered the chain that hobbled him. Though the iron bands still encircled his raw ankles, his feet could move freely.

The boy spoke into Julie's ear, "Take my master's horse. He's swift and strong."

He then disappeared into the mist.

Julie saw the Big One rush into the ring by the campfire, before anyone realized he was free. She flinched, as he twirled the shocked marquis around and, with one mighty blow, knocked him senseless.

Julie was already leading the boy's horse toward Philippe when the Big One leaped astride the marquis' fine horse. Philippe, never bound, jumped on the horse Julie led and pulled her up behind him. They galloped out of the square, as astonished people fell out of their way. The stunned soldiers quickly recovered. "After them, quick! Head them off at the harbor!"

Big One's horse was in the lead. He guided them unerringly toward the shore through the fog, which became thicker as they got nearer the harbor. Philippe followed close behind. In no time, they thundered past a startled guard at the harbor barricade.

"Stop ... stop!" was the guard's futile cry. The rush of their horses flailed him backward into the dirt.

Julie recognized the same pier, or did they all seem alike? They flung themselves from the horses. Big One claimed a sturdy fishing boat. The fisherman protested, weakly, for the desperate, half-naked galley slave was a frightening sight! Julie dug her hand into the moneybag and flung a few pieces of silver at the man's feet. While he scrambled to retrieve his pay, they jumped into his boat.

"Thank God the fog still holds!" breathed Philippe. The well-chosen boat moved swiftly toward open water, while the excited voices from shore became louder. A volley of shot peppered the water several yards away.

Philippe and the Big One pulled on their oars with all their might Soldiers on shore climbed into one fishing boat after another, and shoved off after them. Even if they reached the ship, the soldiers would board it and pull them off. Out of the corner of her eye, Julie saw motion. A conglomeration of fishing boats quickly filled the area between their skimming boat and the shore, clogging the harbor, blocking the soldiers' pursuit. Everywhere fishermen created mass confusion as they shouted at each other, boats bumped together, some even overturning. Soldiers fired their guns into the air and shouted at the fishermen, but the curses of the soldiers fell upon deaf ears. Before the protective fog hid the thwarted soldiers from Julie's view, she saw it would take hours to clear a path to the sea.

Julie turned to face the Big One from her seat in the opposite end of the boat, beside Philippe. The breath of the Big One came in regular gasps, as his muscles rippled over the oars. The boat seemed to fly! He looked up, and their eyes met. He smiled with difficulty, as though it had been a long time since he had tried.

"Do you know where the Floating Gull is anchored?" asked Philippe.

"I do, if she's anchored in her usual position," the Big One replied. He glanced to the northwest and guided the boat first west, then north. At last, he shouted "There she rides."

They raised the oars and waited for the ship to lower a ladder to them. Julie leaned forward and asked earnestly, "Who are you?" Philippe leaned forward, too, listening intently for his answer.

After a breathless moment, the galley slave spoke. "Let me guess who you are, little demoiselle. I pray I am right!" His powerful voice trembled with fresh hope. "Are you the daughter of Jacques de Mirovar?"

Julie nodded. The big man's eyes filled with tears. In a voice so broken it was almost unintelligible, he sobbed, "I am his brother,

Henri."

Julie gasped. Philippe's arm steadied her as he sighed, "Is it possible?"

A rope ladder plopped into the water. Julie, still stunned, climbed up, guided by strong hands. When she reached the top, she rushed to meet her waiting Aubusson friends. Only the children hugged her. The others stood back, embarrassed and confused.

"Auguste told us who you are," explained the blushing Didier.

Julie smiled. "Oh, I'm glad. Now I can be a girl again."

Everyone greeted Philippe with enthusiasm. When the third face appeared, followed by the huge, bare, scarred chest, a shocked silence fell.

Julie looked at his contorted face and ugly scars, pained by the effects of torture on her uncle. His hurt, fiery eyes looked at the group, bewildered. Moving to his side, Julie declared, "This is my uncle, Henri de Mirovar. He's God's latest miracle, sent to guide us safely out of the clutches of our enemies." Then she kissed him lightly on his rough, scarred cheek.

Tears ran down his cheeks, into his beard, as the big man gazed adoringly at Julie. "I often asked God why He didn't take me out of my misery in this world. Now I know why."

The moneybag still held more than enough to purchase passage for all of them, including Henri.

The Floating Gull lifted anchor and set sail. The young Huguenots gathered around De Mirovar and urged him to tell his story.

"When the Bishop of Flanders confiscated our property, I was a hot-blooded youth. The soldiers had dragged my father away in chains. Jacques was comforting my dying mother upstairs when the bishop's men galloped up. I flew into a rage and attacked the soldiers."

He paused, his eyes blank, then continued, "I remember nothing of what I said or did in my fury, but it must have been terrible. When I came to, one of the bishop's men lay dead and others sat covered with bloody bandages. Shackles bound my hands and feet. I never saw any of my family again. I remained in prison for five years and I've been working the galleys for the last eighteen." He shook his great head and looked tenderly at Julie. "When I heard that ranting officer speak of Jacques de Mirovar and his daughter, I wondered if I was finally losing my mind."

As Julie listened, the strain and fatigue of the last several hours caught up with her. She swayed and then felt her uncle's strong arms catch and lift her, gently. "Take her to her cabin," she heard a voice saying.

Jeanne laughed, "We must change our plans. Since Joel is no more, he can't share the boys' bunkers. Mademoiselle will sleep with the girls and me."

Julie vaguely saw the anxious faces of Auguste and Philippe as her uncle reassured them, "She just needs a little rest. Show me where to take her."

When her uncle softly laid Julie on her mattress, she fought through her drowsiness to murmur, "I'm too dirty. I'm a mess." Jeanne brought water and helped her undress and bathe. Jeanne pulled her own nightdress from her bundle and insisted that Julie wear it. She was too tired to resist and sank gratefully into the bunk.

"What time is it?" Julie asked when she opened her eyes much later. Jeanne stood in the doorway.

"You slept all day. It's almost dinnertime. My, you look different," Jeanne exclaimed, shy and self-conscious. "I was really a fool not to guess, wasn't I?" she added, sheepishly.

"If my disguise hadn't fooled everyone, I wouldn't be here now, would I, Jeanne?" she reminded her. "Oh, how glad I am to be a girl again!"

Jeanne turned and rummaged under a bunk. She pulled out her bundle again and lifted a gray gown from it, saying, "You're lucky I brought an extra dress. Now put this on and show our Aubusson family that you really are our Mademoiselle de Mirovar."

Julie looked from Jeanne, still wearing her soiled, bedraggled traveling dress to the simple, fresh frock she held in her hands. "I can't wear your dress, Jeanne. You need it.

"Do you propose to go about the ship in that night gown, Mademoiselle? I'm afraid you have no choice."

Julie sighed. "No, I won't take your only dress. I'll put that masculine garb back on."

Jeanne smiled mischievously. "Oh no, you won't! I don't know where you wore those things after we parted, but their smell was so repulsive, I tossed them overboard hours ago."

Julie laughed. "You win."

"Your hair looks nice, short like that. The dress becomes you."

"You're too kind, Jeanne."

"Now we can call Philippe. I promised to call him as soon as you were presentable." Jeanne moved toward the door.

"No!" Julie stopped her. "He only wants to apologize, Jeanne, and that isn't necessary. In fact, I prefer to avoid that."

"Apologize? Hah! I hope a man will be as eager to 'apologize' to me someday!" teased Jeanne, with a knowing smile.

"Since Auguste told us who you are, everything has fallen into place. I wondered why Philippe acted so harshly toward a lad, apparently without reason. Now I know what his forced hatefulness covered: the love I realized long ago I could never have from Philippe. I'm very happy for you, Julie!"

Julie stared in amazement at the empty doorway through which Jeanne had disappeared. Broad shoulders filled the doorway and there was Philippe smiling down at her. His hands held the bulky tapestry that had never left his back until they boarded the ship. She wished Jeanne hadn't talked as she had, for now she felt embarrassed, too aware of Philippe's presence. Jeanne's notions were preposterous. She no longer thought of him as a grown-up version of her childhood friend. She saw him as a man, real and close enough to touch.

He unfolded the tapestry on the nearest bunk. "Jacques made me promise to deliver this to you aboard ship, Julie," he said without looking up. He stopped after unfolding only a portion. "What?" He held up a wrinkled dress of light blue wool. A warm cape, another two dresses, and other unrecognizable items still lay on the tapestry.

"Lucie! She must have saved these from Mother's things," exclaimed Julie. She took the garment from Philippe. "Won't this be lovely on Jeanne!"

"Jeanne?" Philippe looked puzzled.

"Yes. I like this dress Jeanne gave me, and I want her to have this one."

Philippe looked from the beautifully embroidered gown to the starkly simple dress Julie wore. Julie blushed.

"Yes, I prefer that one, too," he smiled.

They both turned abruptly back to the tapestry. Philippe continued to unfold it. "This must be the secret tapestry he wouldn't let me see," mused Julie, excitement welling up within her. When Philippe tossed back the last fold, they both gasped.

"Jacques! It was Jacques all the time! The mysterious artisan of the great tapestry! Oh, Philippe!"

The tapestry before them was unmistakably the work of the same artist who crafted the tapestry that influenced them so deeply as children. The general composition was the same, but the figures were different. A girl stood protecting, not a bleeding fawn, but a frightened child who clutched a Bible in his hands. The girl's hair was as dark as Julie's, not golden as on the forest lass. The hunter carried not a gun, but an ax. He stood, protecting both the young woman and the child.

"The tapestry speaks, Julie. It carries a message. Look, the wild land in the background must be the wilderness of the New World. The ax is the frontiersman's tool. The Bible signifies Jacques' faith. The child ... look at all the faces," he whispered.

Julie stood transfixed.

"How long had he known my secret?" Philippe wondered aloud.

Julie's throat felt dry as she searched the familiar faces on the tapestry. "Known what secret, Philippe?" she finally stammered.

"I thought I had hidden my secret deeply. I've fought these feelings since I was a gangling youth, laughing at a frolicsome child. The days since you came back into my life have been a torment for me."

She looked wonderingly at Philippe, as he drew her close to him. "That I love you, my dearest, dearest Julie," he whispered.

Julie was so overcome with wonder and love, a love that no longer must be repressed and denied, that she could not speak. She stood still in his arms, not wanting to break the spell that engulfed them.

"Have you no answer for me, Julie?" he insisted, gently.

In answer, she lifted her lips to his eager kiss. When they drew apart, his face showed his unbounded joy. But still she hadn't spoken.

She turned to reach her finger to the tapestry, tracing the handsome features of the frontiersman, unmistakably Philippe. Her finger moved to the tall, slender girl with dark hair, a half-hidden chestnut on her slim neck.

She finally spoke, before moving back into his tender embrace. "My own dear Philippe, at last you understand that I've always wanted to be the girl in your tapestry."

After another moment of deep contentment and joy, they moved apart. Julie saw Philippe's eyes sparkling with mischief.

"Are we to ignore the beautiful significance of the third figure of the tapestry?" he chuckled, as his finger rested on the tapestry's child who was a young likeness of Jacques.

Julie hardly took her eyes from Philippe's face as her own hand settled upon the Bible in the child's hands. "No more than we shall ignore the faith that you're seeking and that I have found. Oh, Philippe, if only Father could know that I am now a believer, as well as that we have found each other!"

"Julie, my love, I can't help but feel that somehow he does know." Philippe rolled up the tapestry, tucked it under his arm, and smiled with love at Julie. "Shall we tell the others?"

"Oh, yes!" she said. "We must show the tapestry to our Aubusson friends, and to our Uncle Henri."

With arms entwined, they left the cabin and walked into the evening light together. The ship sailed straight towards the brilliant sun, towards a new future, a new land. In this new land, they would weave their own tapestry from themes of faith, tolerance, freedom, and love. They would weave this tapestry inspired by the tapestry of their father and assisted by the fugitive Huguenots who were now their only family. They would weave this tapestry – together.

THE END

Historical Postscript:
The Huguenots & Religious Persecution

Long before the Reformation, many French people felt a need for change in the way they worshipped. Protestant leaders presented a new Christian vision which emphasized individual faith and direct access to God through scripture and prayer. Dissatisfied with the often corrupt hierarchy of leadership within the Roman Catholic Church, they desired a simpler, purer form of church government. Many nobles, intellectuals, and artisans converted to this new religion. These French Calvinists called themselves Huguenots.

The powerful Catholic clergy, backed by strong noble allies, bitterly opposed the Huguenots from the beginning. However, the power and attitude of the French king was the major factor which determined how badly Huguenots were persecuted at a given time.

Protestant churches emerged in the early 1520's during the reign of Francis I, who initially buffered them from Catholic extremists. Later in his reign, he began persecutions, which the next several monarchs intensified. In some places, Protestants were burned at the stake as heretics for any outward show of their faith. Owning a French-language Testament was punishable by death. Entire congregations of Huguenots were periodically captured, tortured, and killed, including women and children. Still, Huguenot numbers grew rapidly, reaching several million at their peak. Between 1562 and 1598, religious wars raged between the Catholics and Huguenots, with atrocities committed by both sides. This conflict climaxed in the St. Bartholomew's Day Massacre in 1572, initiated by King Charles IX, in which up to 70,000 Huguenots died treacherously.

The military leader of the Huguenots, Henry of Navarre, crushed a large Catholic force in 1587. Henry was first in line for the throne of France, but was denied the crown until he converted to Catholicism. In 1598 as King, he issued the powerful Edict of Nantes, which granted Huguenots enough religious and other freedom to build their own base of faith, commerce, and power in south and central France.

Louis XIII and Cardinal Richilieu sought to consolidate power in the monarchy, so they crushed the military power of the Huguenots in a 14-month siege of La Rochelle in which 75% of the population died, most of starvation. However, after breaking the Huguenots' military power, they ushered in an era of religious tolerance. The Huguenots thrived in their crafts and businesses. This lasted until 1661 when a young Louis XIV took direct control of government affairs. Under his reign, persecution of Huguenots intensified and became unbearable.

Huguenot children were kidnapped, and dragoons were quartered in Huguenot homes, where they could steal, rape, and pillage without punishment. An informant who reported a family's Huguenot religious affiliation received a third of the family's estate when it was confiscated by the crown. Professions were closed to Huguenots, who were bribed, pressured, and harassed to convert. Louis XIV's policies killed as many as two hundred thousand Huguenots.

The revocation of the Edict of Nantes was the final straw. Up to a million Huguenots fled France, and thousands more died trying. Since most Huguenots were entrepreneurs and artisans, especially in textiles, glass, and china, other countries welcomed them. They contributed to the vitality of many nations including Holland, England, Canada, the U.S., and Germany. Without its Huguenot artisans, the village of Aubusson, famous for centuries for its marvelous tapestries, sank into mediocrity until after World War II when modern artists revived the lost art.

IF YOU THINK THIS BOOK IS GOOD,

IF YOU THINK OTHERS SHOULD READ IT,

DONATE SOME COPIES TO LIBRARIES.

Girl in the Tapestry is the kind of book we want in libraries:
  it tells an exciting story;
  it portrays a wholesome romance;
  it promotes ideals of religious freedom, faith, and family;
  it introduces us to part of our important, little-known heritage.

Buy a copy at your local bookstore and donate it,
or donate through Heartwood Press.

We at Heartwod Press will:
  identify libraries that meet your criteria;
  make sure the libraries will accept and use the book;
  ship the books to the libraries
at a library discount price of $10.00, incl. shipping & handling.

Fill out the form on the other side of this page,
and send it with your check, to:
      Heartwood Press
      3305 Stardust Drive
      Austin, TX 78757
      512-451-5985

I wish my donation of *Girl in the Tapestry* to go to libraries:

____ Wherever the need seems greatest.

Type: ___ school ___ public ___ church other _____

Region _____

State(s) _____

City (s) _____

_____

The following specific libraries:

_____

_____

_____

_____

Other special instructions:

_____

_____

_____

Quantity: _____   Enclosed ($10.00 per book) _____

Copy the above, fill it out, and send to:

Heartwood Press
3305 Stardust Drive
Austin, TX 78757
512-451-5985